1

As always,
Thank you to my family
and friends
for their support
and patience

And thank you, God, for the many
blessings in my life.

Tangled Beauty

K.L. Middleton

Prologue

Michael

She stares down at me and I am lost in those magnificent emerald eyes. They hold me prisoner – a willing captive to this beautiful creature who makes my heart *ache* every time I am in her presence. The desire to taste those sweet lips, and bury myself deep inside of her heat...

It torments my soul.

I struggle to control myself as her hands slide through my hair, ever so lovingly. Her touch, gentle at first, grows bolder as she continues her glorious administrations. Inside, I am groaning with desire as I imagine these able hands wrapped around other parts of my body, followed by her full, succulent lips...

It is almost too much to bear.

I close my eyes and grip the edge of the chair as these wicked thoughts consume me, thankful that my lap is draped in plastic. I try to think of less desirable things, but my body refuses to cooperate, and I am on the edge of control. Just when I think I can no longer contain myself, the faucet is turned off, and she speaks my name...

Michael.

It rolls from her tongue like a lover's caress – so smooth and sexy.

I open my eyes and smile up at this lovely enchantress, wishing I could stare forever at her beauty.

She smiles back and urges me to follow her.

I obey without question as I am quite smitten with this beautiful angel. Truth be told, I would follow her to the depths of Hell if asked. I wouldn't even question it.

I sit down at her station, smoothing the plastic back over my thighs as our eyes meet in the mirror's reflection. She opens her lovely mouth and asks me what I'd like.

I pause.

My pulse is racing and I am brimming with desire. I would like nothing more than to take her, right then and there. To claim her as mine and *mine* alone. To destroy anyone who might interfere or stand in the way of our destiny.

But for now...

I think I'll just settle for a trim.

Chapter One

Sinclair

"Have you heard the news yet?" asked Tiffany.

We were in the back of the salon, mixing hair color.

"What news?" I asked, trying to brush a loose strand of hair away from my eyes without getting any powder in them.

"Judy sold the shop."

I raised my head and stared at her in horror. "What? When?"

"I guess the deal was finalized last night. She sold it to some guy from L.A."

"So, are we getting shut down?"

"No. Nothing's changing but the ownership. She sold it to one of her friend's sons so she could retire."

I heaved a sigh of relief. "Jesus, you scared the hell out of me. I don't know what I'd do if *Tangled* was shut down."

"Me neither. Anyway, I cannot *wait* to meet the owner," gushed the pretty nineteen-year-old. "Judy says he's freakin' hot and that we're all going to love him. He'll be here on Monday."

"Huh," I said, stirring the color. It would be nice having another guy in the shop. I wondered if he knew anything about hair or if he was gay. Many times, it went hand-in-hand.

"Is *that* the color your customer wants?" she asked, pointing towards the swatch I was examining. "It's going to be quite a change for her."

I stared at the bright red lock and nodded. "I've tried talking her out of it, but she keeps insisting."

Tiffany picked up her bowl of color and turned to leave. "Well, good luck with that."

I snorted. "I need more than luck."

My customer, Mrs. Lancaster, was a thick-jowled, heavyset lady in her fifties; a woman who was normally very conservative. Today, she'd brought in a picture of a twenty-something celebrity who had long, vibrant red hair, and wanted *that* same color. Unfortunately, on Mrs. Lancaster, it was going to look like a crime scene.

"Okay," I said, after returning to my station. "You're certain that this is the color?" I asked, holding out the brightly colored strands.

"Yes, dear," she said, touching the sample lovingly between her fingers. "I want that *exact* color. I know it's going to be just lovely."

I forced a smile. "Okay, then. Let's do this."

"Oh, no... oh no, you did not just do that!" hollered Felicia from across the salon.

I turned around and stared at the little old man sitting in Felicia's chair, a huge shit-eating grin on his face.

"Oh, my God," apologized a well-to-do older woman sitting in a chair beside them. "I am so sorry. Henry! You have to behave yourself!"

"No, *I'm* sorry," said Felicia, setting down the scissors. "I am *not* cutting this old man's hair if he's going put his mouth on me. Hell no."

It was then that I noticed the front of Felicia's hot-pink T-shirt. There was a wet spot on her right boob.

"Henry, did you hear that? You have to behave yourself!" scolded the woman. She turned to Felicia. "I am *so* sorry. My brother suffers from Alzheimer's and doesn't always know what he's doing."

I watched the delight in the old man's watery blue eyes and there was no doubt in my mind that he knew *exactly* what he'd done. Felicia was a very top-heavy woman and her breasts sometimes got in the way. She'd even cut my hair once and I was lucky not to walk away with two black eyes.

Felicia picked up her scissors. "Okay, but if he touches me again," she narrowed her eyes. "I'm gonna cut more than his hair."

"Oh, my Lord," whispered my customer. "This is better than daytime television."

I grinned. "You can say that again."

To me, it was just another day at *Tangled*. I'd seen everything, heard everything, and it was what kept me coming back to work every morning. I loved my job, loved my coworkers, and wouldn't trade it for the world.

Fortunately, Henry kept his hands and mouth to himself for the rest of his appointment with Felicia, while I finished coloring and styling Mrs. Lancaster's hair. When it was finished, I turned her back towards the mirror, and held my breath as we stared at the results.

"What do you think?" I asked.

"Oh, my God...it looks fabulous!" she beamed.

I sighed with relief. It still looked shockingly bright to me, but if she liked it, that was all that mattered.

"You look like a new woman," I said, spritzing her hair with hairspray.

She patted the side of her hair fondly. "Mr. Lancaster's idea, actually. He has always *adored* redheads."

I stared at my own auburn hair in the mirror's reflection and wondered if he'd meant something a little more subtle than the 'Ronald McDonald' color she'd selected.

She grabbed my hand and pulled me closer. "Tell me," she whispered. "Do you do pubes, as well?"

"Ah, no," I whispered back. "You're on your own down there."

She bit her lower lip. "Oh, shoot. Maybe I'll just shave it off."

I opened my mouth to reply, but then changed my mind. I certainly did not want to continue that particular conversation.

After she'd paid and left, I rushed to clean my station. I had the weekend off and was going to be spending it on Huntington Beach. I still had a lot of packing to do before the trip and couldn't wait to get started. It was the first time I'd had an entire weekend off in months.

"At least that old geezer gave me a decent tip," declared Felicia, holding up a stack of bills.

"I still can't believe he did that," giggled Tiffany. "What a crazy old coot!"

She nodded and shoved the money into her bra. "The worst thing is, I haven't had *that* much action for almost two months. And then, to get my titty sucked by a toothless old white man?" she clapped her hands and laughed heartily. "Lord, have mercy!"

"Two months?" I snorted. "That's nothing. It's been over a *year* for me."

Her eyes widened. "A year? Girl, next time Henry makes an appointment, we'll make sure *you* get him."

***

"This is never going to work," I told my friend, Jesse, as I slid into his Jag a couple of hours later. "Trust me, we will *never* fool anyone."

He reached over and patted my kneecap. "Sweetie, it *will* work. It *has* to work."

I pulled my hair back behind my ears. "Then you'd better stop calling me 'sweetie' and quit primping yourself every five minutes. You'll never fool your parents if you keep acting like a princess."

Jesse threw his perfectly chiseled face back and laughed. Then he stopped abruptly, and glared at me with faux venom.

I smiled. "Hey, I'm just saying..."

"God, you're such a snotty little bitch."

I shook my head. "No, you've claimed *that* title, honey, and I wouldn't dare try and take it from you."

Glancing into the rearview mirror, he ran his fingers through the top of his short, blonde highlights – the ones I'd given him last night. "And that's why you're my best friend, Sinclair. You know just how to sweet-talk me."

I laughed. "Seriously, though. What were you thinking by inviting me?"

"Well, since it's their twenty-fifth wedding anniversary, they expect me to bring a date of the *female* persuasion. I certainly can't bring Alex, Sin. My parents are assholes. Both of them. They'd never accept the fact that I'm gay and would no doubt freeze up my trust fund if they find found out the truth." He bit one of his fingernails. "And I know it sounds shallow, but I can't live without that money."

I put on my seatbelt. "So, you're just going to keep lying to them? How long do you propose to do that?"

He started the car and the engine purred to life, like an eighty-thousand dollar kitty. "As long as it takes, Sin, as long as it takes."

Forty-minutes later, after listening to him rant about his friends, his career, and his sex life, we finally pulled up to his parents' summer home on Huntington Beach, a luxurious oceanfront property that took my breath away.

"Wow," I breathed, staring at the massive white structure that screamed "Wealth", "Power", and "Dream on, losers!"

"I know," sneered Jesse. "They're disgustingly rich, fortunately for me. But it's also *old* money and even *older* ideals. *Not* fortunate for me."

I'd only known Jesse for eight months, ever since he'd walked into *Tangled.* From the moment he'd plopped his Armani-clad butt in my chair, we'd clicked and I'd become his personal stylist and he, one of my very best friends.

"So, what exactly did you tell them about me?" I asked, feeling nervous now that we were actually going through with it.

The ruse had sounded like fun at the time – a weekend of parties, celebrities, and a chance to escape my own hum-drum life. It had been almost a year since I'd found my ex-fiancé in bed with another woman and I'd basically taken on the habits of a hermit soon afterwards. My life now consisted of work, taking care of my finicky black cat, Felix, and reading trashy romance novels. It was boring and sometimes lonely, but safe, which was what I needed after having my heart crushed by Shawn.

Jesse unwrapped a piece of gum and slid it into his mouth. "Okay, so you and I have been dating on and off for the last six months. Nothing serious yet."

I raised my eyebrows. "Yet?"

"Well, I mean we've fucked and everything," he said, snapping his gum a little too obnoxiously for a twenty-four-year-old.

I feigned a look of shock. "We have? Was it good?"

He puffed out his chest. "Damn right. That's why you won't leave me alone, you crazy, horny bitch."

I laughed and shook my head. "Oh brother, you're so freakin' arrogant."

He blanched. "Arrogant? Gawd... I *hate* that word."

I stared at him and wondered how in the world his parents could think he was anything *but* gay.

"Well, you might want to pretend to be 'arrogant'. That's a trait you'll find on a lot of manly men," I said, deepening my voice.

"Sin, I've *never* been a *manly* man, and my parents have known me all of my life. They just think I'm a very creative and outgoing guy."

I understood that because Jesse really was very creative. He was also a talented graphic designer which, unfortunately, hadn't particularly sat well with his parents. They'd wanted him to become a doctor or lawyer, like his older brother, Reed, who I'd had yet to meet. Supposedly, Reed *was* an arrogant, cocky lawyer who had little time for his younger brother.

"So, you get to act natural while I'm the one who has to be totally enthralled by you?"

He smiled. "Oh, come on. It can't be that difficult. You know you'd 'do me' if I was straight."

13

I rolled my eyes. "Oh, here we go…"

"What? I'd probably 'do you' if I was straight."

"Enough," I said, raising my hand.

He sighed. "Sinclair, you really need to work on your self-confidence. I know it's hard because of what fuck-head did to you, but you really need to get over it. I mean, you're attractive, funny, and have crazy skills when it comes to hair. You're an awesome catch, girlfriend."

"Tell it to the straight guys," I answered dryly.

"Honey, if they can't handle a woman who isn't afraid to speak her mind," he said, "then they certainly don't deserve you."

Jesse was being kind. The fact was that I had a little bit of a temper and sometimes didn't know when to keep my mouth shut, which coincidently, was a trait we both shared. After I'd caught Shawn cheating and kicked him out of our apartment, I'd vowed to never let anyone manipulate or take advantage of me, ever again. So now, if I didn't agree with something someone said, I let them know or if I felt threatened in any way, I usually pounced first. Surprisingly, it sat well with my customers because they kept coming back and asking *me* for advice. Even Jesse had laid his problems out for me, which led to where I was sitting right now – his newest partner in crime.

"How does Alex feel about all of this?" I asked. "Is he still giving you the silent treatment?"

He sighed. "Yes. He's still pissed off that I'm hiding him from my parents. He just doesn't understand. His parents are so freakin' cool, and mine are just... well," he sighed, "mine."

I was having a hard time understanding why he didn't just 'come out'. Jesse had a decent job and his partner, Alex, was *very* well off. The only thing I could fathom was that Jesse's monthly allowance from his trust fund was pretty damn considerable.

"Well, you're going to have to break it to them someday."

"You don't understand how intolerable my parents are, Sin. But," he bit his lower lip, "you will."

"Great, can hardly wait," I answered, now wondering what in the blazes I'd gotten myself into.

We slid out of the Jag and into our roles right away, by strolling hand-in-hand towards the front door, where we were greeted by a very eloquent, grey-haired gentleman.

"Young Mr. Eddington," beamed the older man. "So nice to see you again."

Jessie stood straighter than usual. "Thanks, George," he answered in a slightly deeper tone. "This is my girlfriend, Sinclair Jeffries."

I looked at Jesse, trying to hide my surprise. The transformation from a prima donna to a heterosexual male was comical, considering I knew he hated every minute of it.

One of George's eyebrows lifted as his eyes darted between us. "Charmed to meet you, Ms. Jeffries," he said.

"Same to you," I greeted him. "Just call me Sinclair or Sin."

George's eyes studied both of us for a few seconds and then he nodded. "Very well, Sinclair."

"Crap, I forgot our bags," sighed Jesse. "They're still in the trunk."

"No problem, Mr. Eddington. I'll go retrieve them," said George, holding out his hand for the keys. "Will you be staying in your old bedroom, or," he glanced at me, "one of the guest rooms with Ms. Jeffries, sir?"

"Sinclair," I corrected him.

"Of course," smiled George.

"I'm sure Mimi would prefer that we sleep separately," said Jesse. "So, for *her* benefit, I think we can handle two nights apart."

Deciding to have a little fun, I slid my arm through Jesse's and pouted. "But, Jesse, I don't think I can handle a night without your strong, manly arms around me."

He smiled wickedly. "Now, Sin, I doubt my parents want us banging the headboard against the walls from dusk until dawn. You'll have to live without this guy," he said, pointing down towards his crotch, "for just a couple of days. Then, I'll take you back home and *rock your world*."

I had to bite my lip to keep from laughing. "Okay, but it's going to be so hard, not being together at night."

He slapped my butt. "I'll show you *hard* come Sunday night, lover."

George cleared his throat. "Very well, I will prepare the guestroom for Ms. Jeffries."

"Thank you, George," said Jesse. "Come on, Sin, I'll show you around the palace."

"Okay."

He pulled me away from George, who was still watching us curiously.

"Oh, my God," I whispered, giggling. "I think your butler almost lost his composure there for a moment."

"No, not George. He's used to my brother bringing his trollops over."

"Trollops?"

He rolled his eyes. "Fine, his slutty, gold-digging girlfriends."

I pulled my hair over to the side. "I knew what you meant, goofball. You're just acting so different now that we've entered your parents' domain."

"Sorry," he said, picking a piece of lint off of his light blue Dolce and Gabbana shirt. "Something comes over me the minute I walk into my parents' home. It's like I become an entirely different person. Maybe that's why they don't have a clue that I'm gay. I just can't seem to let myself really go when I'm around them."

I smiled. "Don't worry, Jesse, I can still see the real you behind those baby-blues."

"That's a relief. If I get too stuffy, however, drag my ass out of here."

"You got it, sweetheart," I said, grabbing his hand.

***

Michael

I watched from afar as the young couple strolled up to the front of the house, walking hand-in-hand. It was a good thing I'd been keeping tabs on her the last few days. This was the last place I'd have expected to find her.

And with him?

Tightening my grip on the steering wheel, I fought to suppress my rage, although, it was very difficult – the smiles on their faces made my blood boil.

How could she do this to me?

This *boy* was barely old enough to drive, let alone hold her hand in his, like a familiar lover. It didn't make sense.

She was mine!

I studied his movements as they knocked on the door, and it was then that it hit me.

"Of course," I said out loud, smiling in relief. From the way he carried himself, any idiot could tell he wasn't warming *her* bed at night. They were friends and nothing more. She still fancied me and was obviously waiting for me to make that first move.

18

In time, my love.

I wrote down the address and then started my engine. It was time to start the preparations for our new life together.

Chapter Two

Reed

"Is this seat taken?"

I was lounging in the Marina Bar at LAX, drinking a beer and checking emails on my laptop when I looked up to find a gorgeous blonde smiling down at me. She had a come-fuck-me stare and a cleavage most guys would do anything to get lost in.

Hooker.

I smiled. "Sorry, don't waste your time. I'm happily engaged."

She gave me a pouty look and leaned over the pub table, offering a better view of her tits. "You sure?"

My pants tightened involuntarily. "Yes. Sorry."

Her eyes raked over me appreciatively, and she licked her glossy lips. "Tell you what, handsome, I'll give you a free wedding present. It will be our little secret."

I chuckled. She literally drove a hard bargain. "Thanks, but I really can't."

She straightened up and tossed her hair to the side. "Fine, then. Your loss."

I didn't even bother to respond as her hips swung angrily out of the bar in search of another conquest. Instead, I shut off my computer and thought about my bride-to-be, wondering where the fuck she was. She wasn't returning my calls or texts.

Sela.

I'd only known the twenty-three-year-old French model for six months, but she'd seemed to be everything I'd wanted in a woman – beautiful, sophisticated, and an energetic little wildcat in bed. Unfortunately, she was also spoiled out of her fucking mind with a temper that had already cost me thousands of dollars in china and fine art. The last time she'd freaked out, I'd almost called it quits. But then she'd gotten down on her knees and stared up at me with her pouty lips, begging to suck my cock.

What could any red-blooded American guy say, other than, *"Oui"*?

This week she'd went on another rampage, angry that I'd asked her to fly back to the States to meet my parents. Fortunately, she'd been on the other side of the world when I'd asked, and it hadn't cost me anything but a headache.

Marriage.

Really, what in the hell am I thinking?

Sighing, I tried calling her cell phone once again, with the same irritating results.

***

Sinclair

For the next hour, Jesse showed me around the luxuriously opulent home, pointing out designer wall hangings and furniture pieces that singly cost more than my entire childhood. Most of the décor was contemporary, with white and black as the main color scheme, plus a handful of blue or burgundy pieces thrown in. With all of the white furniture and even whiter, plush carpeting throughout the house, I was afraid to sit, stand, or step on anything.

"Nice and crisp, huh?" remarked Jesse. "That's what comes to mind whenever I visit. You know me – I prefer bright colors, comfortable furniture, and plenty of eclectic pieces. My mother and I have *far* different tastes."

"You say that like it's a bad thing," interrupted an older woman's voice.

We were in the library, *the* whitest library I'd ever seen, and both of us turned to face a tall, thin woman with a silver bob.

"Hello, mother," smiled Jesse.

She walked over to him, grabbed his hands, and air-kissed both of his cheeks. "Jesse, darling. I'm so glad you could make it."

"Me, too. By the way," he said, putting an arm around my waist and reeling me in. "This is my girlfriend, Sinclair Jeffries."

"Yes, you were telling me about her. *Very* nice to meet you," she smiled, although her dark blue eyes regarded me shrewdly. "I'm Mimi Eddington."

I accepted her cool, heavily jeweled hand and shook it. "Nice to meet you, as well, Mrs. Eddington."

"Oh, just call me Mimi. So, Jesse tells me you're a Cosmetologist?"

"Well, yes," I said.

"Do you own your own business, then?" she asked.

I stared at her mouth in awe. She had, what appeared to be, a permanently puckered look – reminding me of someone who'd just tasted a lemon or smelled a bad fart. Staring at her lips, I tried to keep a straight face. "Not yet, but I'm hoping to open my own shop, someday."

She patted her silver hair and smiled. "Well, my stylist, Gigi Sparks, owns a shop in Beverly Hills. She's very successful, although most of her clients are famous, and obviously, that helps."

I smiled. "I've heard of Gigi Sparks, she really is a phenomenal stylist."

"Mm... yes, I agree. Anyway, it just goes to show that anyone can become successful if they work hard and put their mind to it," she said, turning to Jesse. "How's *your* career going, by the way? Still with that quaint, little firm?"

"Blake Designs? Yes, mother, I told you that on the phone last night."

She sighed. "Oh, that's right, I'm sorry. There's so much going on right now, I don't know which end is up."

"Don't worry about it, mom. So, where are Dad and Reed?"

She closed her eyes and rubbed her forehead. "Well, your father is still at the office, and Reed, well, he should be flying in sometime tonight."

"Unbelievable. I still can't believe Reed is making an appearance."

"Your brother is engaged, you know," she said. "A model named Sela Royce."

Jesse's eyebrows shot up. "No fucking way! She must be one good cock –"

"Jesse, please!" gasped Mimi.

He chuckled. "Oh, come on, mom. Reed isn't exactly the marrying type. Is she pregnant?"

Her eyes darted to me and then back over to him. "Of course not," she answered with a disapproving look. "At least," she paused, biting her lower lip. "I don't think so."

He glanced at his nails and shrugged. "Well, you said she's a model? I guess if he was going to settle down with *anyone*, it would be one of those."

Mimi walked over to a book that was sticking out too far on a shelf and pushed it in. "Unfortunately," she said, turning back around, "we may not have the pleasure of meeting her this weekend. She's at a photo-shoot in France. Reed said she was going to try and fly back here sometime today, but I haven't heard from either of them."

"So, you haven't met her either?" he asked.

24

Mimi moved a hand up to her pearls and began twirling them around her finger. "Well, I've spoken to her on the phone before, but other than that, no. Reed has been too busy these last few months. He *is* a lawyer."

I wanted to ask why *that* was relevant, but it wasn't my place and I didn't want to offend anyone.

Jesse didn't care, however. "Well, shoot. If I can make it back here the first weekend of every month, Reed should certainly be able to fit you in, with all of his resources and money."

She pointed to him. "You live less than an hour away and he lives in New York. You, dear boy, should be over more than once a month."

He put his hands on his hips and scowled. "My schedule is busy too, mother. I work over sixty hours a week, you know. It's hard for me to get away, as well."

Right.

Jesse was dating the owner of Blake Designs and the only thing *hard* for him on the weekends, was Alex.

"Well, that's good," she replied. "A hardworking man stays out of trouble."

"Oh, I'm still trouble," he smirked. "Right, Sin?"

I leaned over and gave him a kiss on the cheek. "Definitely."

She turned to me with her puckered look and studied my face. "You know, you look very familiar, have we met before?"

"I don't think so," I answered. I'd never forget a woman with a permanently sour expression.

She raised her finger to her chin and nodded. "I know what it is – you look like that actress, Sophia Loren, when she was a young woman. Are you Italian?"

"I'm not sure," I said. "I was adopted."

She cringed. "Oh, I'm terribly sorry."

I raised my eyebrows. "As far as I'm concerned, there's nothing to be sorry about," I said. "My adoptive parents are wonderful. They've always treated and loved me like I was their own. I'm very blessed to have them in my life."

"Well, that's fortunate. Then you don't hold any hostility towards your birth mom?" she asked.

I shook my head. "No. How can I feel anger towards a woman I've never met? I'm sure she had her reasons."

"Okay," interrupted Jesse, "enough digging into Sin's life. When's dinner?"

"Oh," said Mimi, checking her watch, a diamond-clad Rolex. "Dinner is in an hour. Did you bring something appropriate?" she asked, glancing at my rose-colored peasant blouse and white Levis.

I looked at Jesse. He'd never mentioned anything about a formal dinner on the first night. I'd packed a dress for the party tomorrow, but had selected something more casual for this evening.

"Of course she did," he said, grabbing my arm and stirring me towards the door. "I'm going to show her to one of the guestrooms and we'll meet you down in the dining room at eight o'clock."

She nodded. "Very well. Don't be late."

"Good going," I whispered as he led me away. "You didn't mention I had to wear anything special tonight. I thought this," I waved towards my jeans. "Would be appropriate enough from the way you were talking."

"Sorry, I wasn't thinking. So, um... what about that little black dress you have? I thought you said you were bringing it?" he asked.

"I did, but it's for the party, tomorrow."

He sighed. "We'll go shopping in the morning. In fact, since you're helping me out, I'll even buy you a new dress to wear to the party."

"That's fine by me," I said. "Rent is due next week and my credit cards are almost maxed out."

"If I'm buying, however," he said. "*I'm* picking out the dress, sweetheart. If you're going to be my date, it has to be sexy and over-the-top. I want the other women in the room to be pissed off and the men walking around with gloriously raging hard-ons."

I laughed. "Why does it sound like you're really getting into this?"

He touched the top of his spiky hair and smiled. "Because, even though I'm not going to get laid this weekend, I want everyone in the room thinking that I am."

27

"You're a nut."

"Damn right I am," he smirked. "That's why we get along so good, Sin. I'm completely nuts and you need that in your life right now."

"I won't argue that," I said.

Without Jesse, I'd be alone in my apartment, arguing with my cat, and searching for batteries for my vibrator. This was definitely going to be much more stimulating.

I hoped.

Chapter Three

Reed

"Evening, George."

"Mr. Eddington," nodded George, as I set my overnight bag down. "So nice to see you again."

"And you, as well," I said.

"Dinner will be served in just a few minutes. Would you like me to put your things in your room, so you can join the others?"

"That's okay," I said. "I've got it. I want to change before I eat."

George nodded. "Very good. Will Ms. Royce be joining us this evening?"

I sighed. "Doubt it. The last I heard she was still overseas."

"How unfortunate. You know, Jesse brought a girlfriend this weekend," he said with a sparkle in his eyes.

I raised my eyebrows.

He went on. "Yes, a nice young woman, named Sinclair."

I stared at him for a minute. "You're serious?"

"Oh, yes, Mr. Eddington. They arrived a couple of hours ago."

I rubbed my jaw and smiled. "Interesting. I can't wait to meet her."

"Yes, she's rather lovely."

"I'm sure. Well, this should be a very interesting evening."

"Indeed. Let me know if you need my assistance with anything."

"Thanks, George." I picked up my bag and walked up the white spiral staircase leading to my old bedroom, wondering what the hell was going on with Jesse.

***

Sinclair

Jesse chose the largest guestroom in the house for me and I sighed in pleasure when I saw the awesome view from my balcony. The moment I stepped outside, I imagined myself relaxing in the lounge chair, a drink in one hand, and something steamy to read in the other, listening to the ocean waves. Fortunately, I'd packed the new Kindle my mother had given me for Christmas a couple of months before and planned on using it right before bedtime. That is, if Jesse would allow me any sleep – he'd packed three bottles of our favorite white wine and mentioned drinking some at night on the beach. I'd agreed but only before he dropped the real bomb.

Skinny-dipping.

I shook my head. "Oh no, not this girl."

He grabbed my arm. "Sin, you have to skinny-dip in the ocean at least once in your lifetime. It's so liberating and –"

"Embarrassing! I don't know about you, but I'm not getting caught with *my* pants down."

He shook his head. "Nobody will even see us! I know of *the* perfect spot."

"Well…" I said, mulling it over. The thought of swimming naked in the ocean sounded kind of interesting, although I'd always imagined doing it with a lover, not my gay, faux boyfriend.

"Come on, *live* a little," he prodded. "This is the perfect opportunity. Even better – you don't have to worry about me jumping your bones. You can try it out and if you don't like it, well fine. At least you can say you did it."

I groaned. "Listen, I'll think about it."

"What's to think about? Nobody will see us, I promise! In fact, I'll take you to this spot where my brother used to bring his girlfriends when we were growing up."

"Oh, my God, Jesse, were you spying on them?"

He placed a hand on his chest and shuddered. "Hell no. He told me about it and one night *I* decided to take a swim alone," he lowered his voice, "in fact, it was the first time I went skinny-dipping that I realized I was gay. I'll never forget that night."

I leaned forward, as he'd never mentioned that. "Oh, do tell."

He smiled. "Let's just say our neighbor's nephew, a luscious actor from Chicago, was visiting and, oh, just thinking about him now makes me quiver. Anyway, he straightened out my head and not just the one above my shoulders."

I giggled. "Seriously? How old were you?"

With a faraway look in his eyes, he sighed wistfully. "I was eighteen and he was in his twenties. It was one of the most memorable nights of my life. Funny thing is, he's insanely famous now and nobody would suspect him of being bisexual."

He then told me the actor's name and I had to pick my jaw up off the ground.

"No freakin' way!"

"I know. Too bad it only happened once. It certainly helped change the course of my life, though. It was one of the only fond memories I had living under my parents' roof."

"It was? Oh, Jesse," I sighed. "Well, then we'll definitely have to celebrate that memorable occasion with a glass of wine and a quick midnight swim. Who knows, I might even get the courage to remove my bathing suit."

He grinned. "I'll even promise not to vomit if I see your 'fun-bags'."

I rolled my eyes. "You're so crude."

"Thank you."

I pointed towards the door. "Now leave, or you'll see much more of me than you ever wanted."

"Thanks for the warning," he said, moving quickly towards the door. "I'll be back for you later."

As I unpacked the black dress, my thoughts drifted to Mimi. She was a little tightly wound, but not quite as bad as I'd originally expected. Of course, I'd never lived with her and couldn't imagine having a mother who gave me "air-kisses." I thought about my own parents – Ben and Mary Jeffries. They were kindred souls, both warm, loving, and would give you the shirt off of their backs to make you feel welcomed in their home. I loved them dearly and wouldn't give them up for the world. Not for anything. As far as my biological parents were concerned, I was open to meeting them, but I certainly wasn't in any kind of hurry.

I slipped on the form-fitting dress and stared at myself in the mirror. Long auburn hair, curves, round booty, and lips that I'd always thought were much too full. In fact, when I was a teenager, I'd tried to find ways to make them appear smaller, especially after Billy Davis had teased me at party with a cruel comment, telling everyone that I had "cock-sucking lips." I'd been mortified at the time, and even to this day, still felt a little self-conscious about them. When I'd confided all of this to Jesse and had talked about having them reduced, he'd looked at me like I'd lost my mind.

"Women have their lips filled with collagen to get what you already have, honey. Don't you *dare* touch those cock-sucking lips."

Thus, I hadn't touched them, but neither had anyone else in the last year. Needless to say, hanging out with Jesse and hearing about his sexual exploits was beginning to drive me crazy. I was over Shawn but found myself fantasizing about sex in the most inopportune times – when I was running my hands through a sexy male customer's hair, searching through the meat aisle in the grocery store, or at the gym while I watched the muscle-heads lift weights. With their straining biceps, tight buns, and flushed faces, it was enough to make me squirm on my stationary bike. Needless to say, I was frustrated and sometimes jealous of all the penis Jesse was getting. I just wasn't courageous enough to do anything about it yet.

Pushing these thoughts out of my mind, I slipped on my black heels and waited for him.

"Ready?" asked Jessie, fifteen minutes later, wearing a dark gray wool suit.

"Yes. Wow, you look so polished and handsome." I smiled.

He lifted his chin in the air and posed. "Saks, Armani."

I sighed, put my hands on my hips, and posed. "Kohl's, discount rack."

He burst out laughing and grabbed my hand. "Doesn't matter, you still look good, even with that obnoxious cleavage."

I looked down. "Obnoxious?"

"Oh, I'm just giving you shit," he said, pulling me out of the bedroom. "I'm sure you're every heterosexual man's wet dream in that dress, Sin. Take a chill pill."

"Thanks, I think."

When we arrived in the dining room, Mimi and an older man who shared Jesse's bright, blue eyes were already waiting.

"Oh, good," said Mimi. "They're on time."

Jesse's father stood up as I prepared to sit next to Jesse at the dining table. "Ms. Jeffries," he smiled warmly, holding out his hand. "I'm Jesse's father, Jack Eddington. It's a pleasure meeting you."

"Nice meeting you, too. Please call me Sinclair," I answered, as his hand clasped mine.

His eyes raked over my body and he licked his lips. "Well, I'm pleased to see that Jesse also has exquisite taste in women. Just like the rest of the Eddington men."

I blushed. "Well, thank you." I smiled.

He released my hand and motioned for Jesse to pull out my chair. "Son?"

"Oh, where *are* my manners?" quipped Jesse, as he stood back up and pulled it out for me.

"Thanks, babe." I smiled back at him as he pushed my chair.

"You're welcome, *lover*," he answered, tugging on a strand of my hair.

"Sinclair, would you care for a glass of wine?" asked Jack. "We have a bottle of Chateau Margaux that I just opened for Mimi. How is it, by the way, my dear?" he asked.

Mimi, who'd just taken a prim sip, retained her puckered expression and nodded. "Yes, a little dry, but good."

"Sin *adores* wine," drawled Jesse, grabbing the bottle.

"Good, she'll fit right in here," said Jack.

Jesse poured both of us a healthy glass and took a sip. "Oh, yes," he groaned in pleasure. "This wine could definitely cause a scandal. Honestly, I could see myself drinking a case of this."

Jack smoothed down the right side of his moustache and smirked. "At seven thousand a bottle, I highly doubt we'll have to worry about that little exhibition."

Jesse burst out laughing. "Oh, contraire. I know where you hide the booze and I also know you can certainly afford it. How is the casting business, by the way?"

From what I'd understood, Jack was some bigwig casting director and made mucho dollars. Another reason why many celebrities were expected at tomorrow's party.

He tilted his head and looked down at his own drink. "Well, actually, I'm considering retiring."

Jesse's eyes widened. "You're kidding,"

"Not at all," said Jack, swirling the ice around in his glass. "I've had enough of the political bullshit and would much rather spend my days playing golf or sailing on the yacht." He looked at me. "Do you sail?"

I cleared my throat. "Unfortunately, I've never been sailing."

He smiled. "Well, I'm sure we can remedy that. What do you say, Jesse? Invite her over again, next weekend and we'll de-virginize her."

Jesse choked on his sip of wine.

I patted his back and murmured, "What's wrong Jesse? Never de-virginized a woman before?"

"Who's a virgin?" interrupted a deep, velvety voice.

All three of us turned to stare at the tall, dark-haired man standing in the doorway. As he moved closer, my breath hitched and something inside of me woke up – a desire to be naked and staring up into the most intense blue eyes I'd ever seen.

Wow, I had no idea Jesse's brother was so freakin' hot.

"Oh, Reed!" gushed Mimi, standing up. "Come here and give your mother a hug!"

I whipped my head back to Mimi, who stared at her older son as if he was some sort of god. It made me sick to my stomach to see her treat two sons so profoundly different.

Reed gave her a hug, shook his father's hand, and then turned to Jesse. "Look at you, all 'dressed to the nines'. You make me look like a bum off the streets," he said, motioning towards his dark jeans and yellow polo shirt. With perfectly chiseled features, broad shoulders, and athletic build, I couldn't imagine any bum looking quite like that.

"Oh, you look just fine," said Mimi. "Sit down and join us, Reed. We were waiting for Gretchen to serve dinner. In fact," she said, moving towards the door. "Let me see what is taking so long."

As she left to check on the food, I stole another glance at Reed's face, noting that his nose appeared like it may have been broken once or twice and he had a small white scar under his lip. These things seemed to make him even more hot and I wondered if he'd gotten them fighting. Jesse had mentioned that his brother had been a hothead in high school.

He caught me checking him out and smiled a deeply dimpled one that warmed my tummy.

What in the hell was wrong with you, he's taken and you're definitely not looking, I told myself.

"Son, introduce your girlfriend," said Jack, finishing off his cocktail. "Where are your manners?"

Jesse, who had just taken a bite out of a piece of bread, waved his hand. "Oh, yeah – Reed, Sin, Sin, Reed."

"Sin?" asked Reed, a corner of his mouth twitching as our eyes met, again.

I raised my chin. "It's short for Sinclair."

"Don't let that fool you," said Jesse, with a wicked grin. "She lives up to her name."

I elbowed him in the ribs and he grunted.

"So, girlfriend, huh?" remarked Reed, lifting the bottle of wine and studying it. "I had no idea you had a woman in your life."

"There are many things that you don't know about me," said Jesse, examining his nails again.

Reed chuckled. "I guess so. Tell me, Jesse, how long have you been hiding Sinclair from us?"

"Actually, we've only been dating for a short time," he said.

"Interesting," he said, pushing the wine aside. "So, how did you two lovebirds meet?"

"We met at *Tangled*," said Jesse. "She's the top hair designer at their salon."

I turned to Jesse and raised my eyebrows. I was good, but far from being their "top" hair designer.

Reed ran a hand through his sandy-brown hair and smiled. "I could use a haircut, maybe I should make an appointment."

Jesse pointed up to his highlights. "She just foiled me yesterday. You should consider getting a little splash of color thrown in to yours."

Reed turned to me, his eyes probing mine. "What do you think, Sin?"

"I don't think you should change it," I said, wondering if his hair was as soft as it looked. "It's a good color on you."

He looked back over to Jesse. "Good, because personally, I feel that if someone doesn't like me for who I am – fuck 'em."

"Easy for you to say, Reed," replied Jesse. "You've never had to prove yourself to anyone. Even now, with that stubbly mug of yours, you're still larger than life."

Reed rubbed the dark shadow on his chin and smiled. "Larger than life, huh? Listen, Jesse, there's only one person I need to prove anything to," he replied, sitting back in his chair. "Myself."

"Right," said Jesse.

"No, it's true. It's the *only* way to live, man. Otherwise you'll spend your entire life beating yourself up for the sake of others."

Jack cleared his throat. "Not to change the subject, but where is that lovely fiancée of yours, Reed?"

A flash of irritation passed through his icy eyes. He shrugged. "Guess she couldn't make it."

"Uh oh," smirked Jesse. "Trouble in paradise?"

Reed's lips thinned. "Let's just say, little brother, which I'm sure you've learned, some women are predictable but most are... unpredictable."

"Oh," I interrupted, suddenly feeling very defensive of my gender. "Interesting assessment of women, which one is your fiancée?"

"The disappointing kind, she's far *too* predictable."

"Too predictable, huh? How so?" I asked, unable to help myself. Another man thinking that *he* knew all about women. Now *that* was predictable.

Reed, obviously sensing my disapproval, stared at me with amusement. "Let's just say she's a temperamental, spoiled little rich girl, who's always gotten her way, and if things don't go exactly as planned for her, she will make your world miserable."

"Sounds like the perfect woman," replied Jesse. "You must have searched far and wide for this delightful little creature."

40

"More like collided," said Reed.

"So, when is the wedding?" I asked.

Before he could answer, Mimi stepped back into the room. "Dinner is on its way and good news – Sela made it! She's freshening up and will be down shortly."

"Wonderful," muttered Reed, grabbing the wine and filling his glass. Tapping out the very last drop in the bottle, he looked at Mimi. "We'd better keep these coming."

Chapter Four

Reed

As I left the dining room, I thought about Sinclair. Not only was she drop-dead gorgeous, with those heart-stopping green eyes, the cascade of reddish-brown hair, and unforgettable lips, but obviously a feisty little wench. I wasn't sure what kind of relationship my brother had with her, but I knew one thing – it definitely wasn't sexual. A satisfied woman wouldn't have undressed me with that kind of hunger in her eyes. Not like Sinclair had.

Besides, my brother was so gay, he couldn't even think straight.

Chuckling to myself, I went upstairs to search for Sela and found her in one of the five guestrooms, standing over a suitcase in nothing but a hot pink pushup bra and lacy thong panties.

I cleared my throat. "Looks like I arrived just in time."

She turned around, her eyes blazing. "I don't know about that," she snapped, raising her arms in the air in frustration. "Thank you, by the way! I had to meet your mother all by myself, without any kind of introductions."

I frowned. "Look, I didn't know you were coming. In fact, I've been trying to reach you all day. What happened; did your phone fall out of the plane?"

"Ha-ha, funny man. No, it died," she said, turning back to her suitcase. As she bent over to look through her things, all I could think about was burying myself deep inside of her. Then, when she dropped a hairbrush on the floor and reached down to pick it up, it was too much. I moved in behind her, slipping one hand between her legs, the other on her perky little breast. "We could skip dinner and have dessert," I breathed, nibbling on her earlobe.

She slapped my hands away. "Reed," she warned. "There's no time for this."

Groaning with two weeks of pent-up frustration, I turned her around and pulled her to me, sliding my hands over the curve of her ass. "Come on, I haven't seen you in almost two weeks. I'm ready to explode."

"Not... my... fault..." she said, pushing me away. "You could have flown out to see me."

I sighed. "You know why I couldn't. I had to be in court all week."

"Right, your cases," she sneered, slipping a cream-colored dress over her head. "You know, if I knew you were going to spend so much time in 'court', I would have put more thought into marrying you."

"You're being ridiculous. Obviously I just can't pick up and leave whenever I want to."

She grabbed her lipstick and turned towards the mirror on the wall. After applying a generous amount to her lips, she glared at me. "There's always an excuse, isn't there?" she said, then lowered her voice to mimic mine. "I have a case I'm working on, I have to do some research, I have an interview." She turned around. "Well, what about me? When do I get any of your precious attention?"

"Look, Sela, if you weren't traveling around the country all the time, you'd see me every morning and night."

"Oh, now it's *my* fault," she huffed.

I sighed. "No, I'm not saying that. Look, we both had these careers before we met. We *both* knew what we were getting ourselves into."

"No, I didn't because *you* pursued *me* and we spent much more time together. Now, I'm beginning to think that there is someone else who is taking up more of your time."

My eyebrows shot up. "What?"

She raised her chin. "A lover, perhaps?"

"That's bullshit," I snapped. "There is nobody else, for Christ's sake. I can't believe you're accusing me of that."

"Really? I heard you were quite the... the... ladies' man, before me."

"That was then," I said. "Now I'm a happily engaged man."

With a seductive smile, she slipped her arms around my neck. "If there is anyone else, Reed, and I find out," she murmured, her French accent thicker than usual. "I'll cut off your deeck."

"My deeck?" I put her hand on my straining zipper. "Sela, there *is* nobody else," I said. "So do me a favor – either stop with the accusations, or do something more useful with that mouth."

She licked her lips and slid down to her knees. "Something more useful?" she whispered, unzipping my pants.

I sucked in my breath as she pulled out my cock and slid it between her lips.

"Is this what you meant?" she asked, licking the tip.

I groaned. "That'll work."

Chapter Five

Sinclair

"Sela is certainly lovely," said Mimi, placing a napkin on her lap. "I can understand why Reed is so smitten with her."

"So, she's not pregnant?" asked Jesse.

"Jesse..." she warned with a withering stare.

"What? It's a sincere question," he replied.

Mimi didn't respond. Instead she bit into her salad and glanced towards Jack, who was furiously texting on his cell phone.

"Well if she is, we'll know soon enough," replied Jack, looking up. "Anyway, Reed is twenty-seven. He's definitely old enough to settle down."

"I wonder how long they've been dating," said Jesse. "If she's some big-time model, I would have thought I'd have read something about them in the tabloids."

"Reed detests the paparazzi," sniffed Mimi, "especially after dating that actress a few years back, the one who tried using him to get in with your father. After he dumped her, she made all of those vile accusations about him and made Reed look like some kind of arrogant baboon."

"What kind of accusations?" I asked.

Mimi waved her hand. "Oh, that he had a horrible temper, drank too much, and was a womanizer."

"And those weren't true?" snorted Jesse.

"Hardly. Your brother does not have a drinking problem," said Mimi. "It's absurd."

"But the rest is true?" I asked, biting back a smile.

"Well, I'm sure that creature brought out the worst in him," replied Mimi. "She was a dreadful girl. Don't you agree, Jack?"

He looked up. "Despicable. But, unfortunately, she got what she wanted. Notoriety. She was even cast in a couple of movies soon after."

"Seriously?" I asked.

Jack shrugged. "Yeah, but they were 'B' movies."

I worked on my salad and was almost finished when Reed and Sela stepped into the dining room. As they moved closer, I stared at her and sighed; she was everything I wasn't – tall, rail-thin, with light blonde hair, high cheekbones, and perfect little bow-shaped lips.

Reed introduced her to all of us and then they sat down across from me and Jesse.

"I'm sorry I'm late," she said with a slight French accent.

"Oh, it's quite all right," gushed Mimi, staring at her future daughter-in-law with appraisal. "You have a busy schedule. I'm just happy you were able to make it."

"Yes, it is... upsetting, having to travel so much," said Sela. "I never get any rest."

"Or time to eat?" joked Jesse, under his breath.

47

I kicked the outside of his foot.

"You should really take some time off," said Reed, pouring Sela a glass of wine.

Sela's eyes narrowed. "As I've mentioned before, *Reed*, I simply cannot do that. You know that I've already committed myself for the fashion shows in Paris. Maybe *you* should take some time off to be with me."

"I can't take time away from my cases, unfortunately," he replied. "People's lives are depending on me."

"People's lives depend on me, too, Reed," she answered, tightly.

"Well, we are delighted that you could make it here this weekend," interrupted Mimi, obviously sensing the tension. "Right, Jack?"

Jack, who was smiling down at his phone, looked up. "Right, Mimi."

"For Heaven's sake, would it hurt you to put that thing away for a little while?" she chastised. "I'm pretty sure the studio will live without your attention for the next hour."

Jack chuckled and stood up. "You'd think, wouldn't you? Please excuse me, everyone. I need to make a quick phone call. Be right back."

Mimi frowned. "Jack –"

"Feel free to start the main course without me if it takes too long," he said, hurrying off.

Mimi stared at Jack's retreating back, lost in her own thoughts, and something told me that theirs wasn't the perfect marriage.

"I see some things never change," murmured Jesse under his breath.

"So," said Reed, pouring himself another glass of wine. "Where is your shop located?" he asked me. "I think I'll make an appointment this week."

"It's in Midway City," I said, "near the art museum."

"Reed, I thought you were flying back to New York with *me* on Sunday?" asked Sela.

He shrugged. "Actually, I have some business I need to take care of in Stanton. Plus, I haven't been home in a while. You don't mind if I stick around for a few days, do you, mother?"

Mimi's face lit up. "Are you serious? That would be marvelous."

Sela looked across the table at me. "So, what kind of shop do you have?"

"I'm a hairstylist," I replied. "I work for *Tangled.*"

"*Tangled*?" She looked up at my hair. "Do you cut and style your own hair?"

"No. I leave that up to my coworkers. I *have* cut and colored Jessie's, however. Many times."

From the haughty look that flashed through her eyes, she was far from impressed. She turned to Reed. "Reed, if you really want your hair done right, I recommend Milan. He is *my* personal stylist."

"Excuse me?" retorted Jesse, with a look that would melt an iceberg in less than a second. "What is that supposed to –"

"No, I think I'd like to give Sin a try," interrupted Reed. "I have faith in her abilities."

I grinned. "I'd love to give you a haircut. In fact, I brought my scissors. I can cut it before tomorrow's party if you'd like?"

He smiled broadly. "I'd really appreciate that. Thank you."

"No problem," I said and turned to Sela. "You know, I can touch-up your hair a little, as well. Even out some of those areas that Milan seems to have missed."

Jesse pointed towards her head. "He did, look over to the right. She should really get that fixed."

"My hair is fine," snapped Sela, glaring at the both of us. "It is supposed to look like this."

"Oh, of course," I answered with a wide-eyed grin.

"I'm sure it's all the rage in Paris," smirked Jesse.

"It is," said Sela, twirling her massive engagement ring around on her finger angrily. "Of course, we are usually ahead of you in regards to fashion and style."

"Clearly," said Mimi. "You look very lovely, dear."

"Thank you," replied Sela. "Obviously, you have great taste."

Jesse and Reed talked about their careers during dinner while the rest of us sat silently. Then, as Gretchen served our main course of prime rib, Spinach Rockefeller, and some kind of delicious finger potatoes, Sela proved to be even more viscous.

"I'll just have a little of the spinach," said Sela, as Gretchen tried offering her some of the prime rib.

I stared down at my plate of food, which had healthy portions of everything.

What can I say? I like to eat.

Sela noticed my plate of food and sneered. "You should reconsider. Eating like that makes a girl fat."

Before I could respond, Reed said, "Actually, Sela, you should consider eating *more* food. You're getting much too thin. It isn't healthy."

She gave him a scathing look. "I'm a model. *I* can't afford to look fat."

I cleared my throat. "Actually, I should probably stick to smaller portions myself," I said, thinking about the extra few pounds I'd put on in the last year. I still needed to lose those before I'd feel comfortable in any kind of bathing suit.

"Nonsense," said Jesse. "You look great. You obviously know how to eat right."

"Oh, I think we can all agree that Sinclair knows what she's doing," piped in Jack, his eyes glossy as he stepped back into the dining room, swaying slightly. "If she fills out a swimsuit as well as she does that dress..."

"Jack!" gasped Mimi.

"Oh, chill out, Mimi," said Jack with a lopsided grin. "You still fill out your swimsuit nicely too, my dear."

Mimi smiled, her cheeks pink. "Oh, Jack."

"Speaking of swimsuits," said Jesse. "Sin and I were thinking of leaving ours here and going for a little skinny-dip in the ocean around midnight. Anyone else game?"

"Seriously?" asked Reed, raising an eyebrow.

I shook my head vehemently. "No, he's just kidding."

"The hell I am," spouted Jesse. "We're going to that spot you used to bring all your women, Reed."

Sela's eyes narrowed. "Your women? When was that?"

"Don't worry, it was long before you," said Reed, patting her hand.

"I'd join you, but something tells me I'd get in trouble from *the* boss," chuckled Jack as he nodded towards Mimi.

"Don't you *dare* go skinny-dipping anywhere on the beach," said Mimi with a look of horror. "None of you. I simply forbid it."

Jesse waved his hand. "Oh, you're so paranoid, mother."

"Sounds like fun," smiled Sela. "I love skinny-dipping."

"And you're French," said Jesse. "You people love walking around nude, flaunting your bodies."

"Because we know how to eat right and take care of them," she said, again staring directly at me. "We have nothing to be ashamed of."

I thought about drowning her in the ocean and wondered if skinny girls sank or floated in saltwater.

Mimi shook her head, still upset. "Goodness, I can't believe any of you are actually considering this."

"Mother, it's in a spot where nobody will even notice us," said Jesse.

"But it must be someone's private property. What if they catch you?" asked Mimi.

"Then we'll just have to ask them to join us," joked Jesse.

"I don't want to know anything more," said Mimi. "The less I know, the better."

"So, are you in or out, Reed?" asked Jesse.

"He is in," replied Sela.

Jesse raised his wine glass. "Then here's to swimming with the sharks. Hopefully none of our bobbers catch a bite."

"Sharks?" I gasped.

Chapter Six

Reed

After dinner, Sela suddenly claimed to have developed a raging headache as I followed her back to the bedroom.

"It's been a long day," she said, sitting down at the edge of the bed. She closed her eyes. "You know, Reed, I think I would just like to take a bath and go to sleep. No swimming."

I sat down next to her and began rubbing her slender, tan shoulders. "After a ten-hour flight, I'm sure you're exhausted."

She sighed. "Mm... yes."

I kissed the back of her neck. "Why don't I run you a bath and join you?"

She shook her head. "No. Not with this pain." She raised her hands to her temples. "I think it's turning into a migraine."

"Take some aspirin."

She turned around and looked at me like I was an idiot. "I need something stronger than that. It's a *migraine*."

"Right. Well, I'm sure my mother has something stronger," I said, standing up. "I'll go check with her."

She smiled. "Thank you."

I went upstairs to my parents' bedroom, and was about to knock when I heard them arguing on the other side.

"It was her, wasn't it?" hollered my mother. "You're still with her – don't lie to me!"

"Mimi, I don't have time for this," snapped Jack. "I told you I stopped seeing her over a year ago."

She laughed bitterly. "Why should I believe you?"

Backing away from the door, I turned around and left. It was the same old song and dance with my stepdad, Jack, not being able to keep his dick in his pants. I learned years ago to just stay the hell out of it. The worst thing was – she'd always known about his escapades, even before they were married, yet she remained with him. If she couldn't see he'd never change, then that was her problem. I wasn't about to get involved, I had enough on my plate with Sela's emotional meltdowns.

When I arrived back at the room, she was lying against the pillows, talking on her cell phone.

"I have to go," she murmured, looking up. "I'll see you when I fly back."

"Who was that?" I asked when she dropped the phone onto the bed.

She shrugged. "My agent."

"Oh. Well, unfortunately, I couldn't find anything stronger for that migraine. Do you have some kind of a prescription for those types of headaches?"

She scooted to the edge of the bed and stood up. "Not here. Don't worry about it, Reed. Once I finish my bath and get some sleep, I'm sure I will feel better."

I walked over and pulled her into my arms. "Are you sure you don't want me to join you?"

Her cell phone began to vibrate.

She pushed me away, grabbed the phone, and read the message, her lips curling up in pleasure.

"What, did you win another free movie rental?" I asked dryly.

"No. Just my agent, again. She's keeping me up-to-date on things."

Her agent was a raging bitch named Delia LeFevre. She didn't care much for me, and the feeling was mutual. Ever since I'd asked Sela to marry me, she'd been trying to talk her out of it. Claimed I was a player and would break her heart. But that was bullshit. I *was* a player, but that was before I'd slid my ring on Sela's finger. Unlike my father, I was determined to be faithful and make our marriage work.

"Wonderful," I muttered. "She'll be bugging us all weekend, I'm sure."

She studied me for a minute and then shoved the phone into her purse. "Reed, could you draw me a bath?" she asked, moving towards me. She slid her arms around my waist and rested her cheek against my chest. "Please?"

"Of course," I said, rubbing her back.

"Thank you, my love."

I raised my eyebrows. *Love* wasn't in Sela's vocabulary. The only time she ever mentioned the word was when I went down on her.

"Hey," I said, tilting her chin up so I could stare into her eyes. I smiled. "I've really missed you."

"Me too."

Something about her response didn't sit well. I wondered if she was still angry with me. "Is there anything wrong?" I asked.

She shook her head. "No, why?"

"You just seemed a little distant."

"It's been a long day."

"You'd tell me if there was anything wrong?"

She shrugged. "Of course."

Staring into her eyes, I lowered my mouth and kissed her softly. As I slid my tongue between her lips, she pulled away. "Reed, please... the bath?"

I sighed. "Fine."

She opened up a smaller suitcase and handed me a bottle of bubble bath. "Thanks."

I went into the bathroom and began filling the tub, pouring some of the pink liquid into the water. I thought about her body, wet and glistening with suds, and decided to try one last time to persuade her into letting me wash her back. Putting the bottle down, I turned and walked back into the bedroom. "What in the hell are you doing?" I demanded, stopping in my tracks.

She lifted her face from the line of white powder and rubbed her nose. "What does it look like?"

I clenched my jaw. "You said you gave that shit up."

"I did, but…"

"But what?"

She stared at me for a minute and sighed. "For God's sake – what's the big deal? I'm an adult. I shouldn't have to explain this or answer to anyone."

I grabbed the tray of coke and stormed back into the bathroom.

"Reed!" she hollered, moving behind me, trying to grab my arm. "Give that back. I wasn't finished!"

"Oh," I sneered," yes, you were."

"Reed!"

I shook my head. "No, Sela, absolutely not. Not this shit, not here and definitely, not you."

"You can't tell me what to do!" she cried.

I emptied it into the toilet and flushed it. "Bullshit," I said, slamming the lid down. "You know how I feel about drugs. We talked about this *many* times before!"

"*You* talked about it," she hollered back, walking out of the bathroom. "I never promised anything."

I followed her. "Obviously I was the only one coherent during that particular conversation. Sela," I said, grabbing her by the shoulders, "listen, I f*orbid* you to even consider doing that shit again, or *any* drug for that matter. You got that?"

She tried pushing me away. "Let me go."

"Look at me," I demanded. "Promise me that you'll stop."

"No, I won't," she said. "I only do it once in a while and... it helps me concentrate."

"Helps you concentrate? That's bullshit! Sela, you know that shit is not allowed in my parents' home or in our home, for that matter."

"Well, then maybe we shouldn't ever live together," she said, glaring up at me.

Her words crushed me. I released her. "You'd honestly choose drugs over me?"

She raised her chin defiantly. "No, but what I do choose is *my* freedom to decide what *I* want to do. I'm not a child and nobody will tell me the way to live my life. Not you or anyone else."

I was so pissed, I wanted to throttle her. Instead, I decided to get the fuck out before I did something I'd surely regret. As I moved towards the door, she called after me.

"What?" I snapped.

She smiled sadly. "You're being unreasonable."

"Is that right?"

"Yes, just stop this, please."

I sighed. "Sela..."

"Don't leave me," she pouted. "I don't like being alone."

"You're not a child, huh? You're certainly acting like one. You'd better think about your choices in life because I'm dead serious about the drugs, Sela. If you won't give them up, then there is no way in hell it will work between us."

She gave me a murderous look before she stormed back into the bathroom and slammed the door.

Chapter Seven

Sinclair

"I still can't believe I let you talk me into this," I said, zipping up my turquoise hoodie. "It wouldn't have been so bad if it would have just been the two of us, but now..."

"Oh, relax," said Jesse. "You have to let loose and live a little."

"But, your *brother* is going to see me naked!"

"It will only be for a second," he said. "All you have to do is strip and make a dash for the water."

"Right," I said, picturing how my boobs would be swaying back and forth in a most unflattering way.

"You know, that Sela is a total cunt," said Jesse. "If I was a woman, I'd kick her bony ass back to France. I don't understand why Reed has such a hard-on for her."

"She's certainly pretty enough," I said. "He must just be totally enamored by her looks."

He wrinkled his nose. "If you can see past that stone-cold bitchiness."

"Well, she must have some hidden talents that keep Reed happy."

"Girlfriend, pu-lease. Even if she sucks cock better than me, she's still not worth the gas it took the cabbie to drop her ass off at our doorstep."

I chuckled. "Well, she's going to be your sister-in-law," I said. "You'll have to somehow learn to accept her."

"No, I don't, and you know why? Because she won't be around long enough to bother," he said. "Reed will come to his senses and kick her to the curb. I'll give them six months."

"That much?"

"Okay, three," he said, tossing me a beach towel.

I stared down at it and sighed. "Why are we doing this again?"

"It's liberating, exhilarating, and totally naughty," he grinned wickedly. "You'll love it."

I didn't know about that. Being naughty was his thing, not mine. "Let's just get it over with," I mumbled, following him out of my bedroom.

It turned out that all of my fears were for naught. We arrived at the private alcove just before midnight and there was no sign of Reed or Sela.

"It's beautiful," I said, staring at the low tide under the moonlight. It looked so tranquil, so peaceful. Now, that I was actually here, I was glad I'd been talked into coming.

"Spread out the towels and we'll have a nightcap before we strip and run around naked."

"I'll need it."

As we enjoyed the wine, Jesse stared towards the ocean, a wistful look on his face. "It seems like yesterday..."

I smiled. "What, that you were swept off your feet by that actor?"

He took a sip of wine. "Yes. I was so confused until that night, Sin," he said, turning to me. "I mean, I tried, I really did, to be what everyone else wanted me to be. I even went out on a couple of dates with girls, but it always felt so wrong."

"What, like kissing a brother or sister?"

He laughed. "Probably. I don't know; I've never kissed Reed before."

I hit him playfully in the shoulder. "You know what I mean, smartass."

"Yeah. Anyway, I guess deep down I always knew I was gay."

"Did you ever try talking to anyone about it?"

He sighed. "Once. My parents invited this couple over and they had a son, who was the same age as me, I think we were seventeen at the time. Anyway, I thought for sure he was gay and when I broached the subject, he literally freaked out."

"What happened?"

He smiled bitterly. "Called me a few names and then took a swing at me. He went completely berserk."

"Why did he freak out so bad? Did you make a move on him or something?"

He rolled his eyes. "No. I just told him that I was confused about girls and whether or not they were for me. Then I asked him if he'd ever been with a guy before, and he acted like a total asshole."

"That's too bad."

He nodded. "You know what the worst part is?"

I took a sip of wine. "What?"

"He came out of the closet."

My eyebrows shot up. "You're kidding."

"Not at all. My parents mentioned it a couple of years ago. They were obviously flabbergasted about the entire thing." He scowled. "My parents are so homophobic, it's pathetic."

"Well, I think that guy owes you an apology."

He took a drink of his wine. "At the very least," he said. "But really, I don't care. He was obviously battling his own feelings at the time. Although, once an asshole, always an asshole. Speaking of..."

I turned to see where he was looking and felt a warm rush swirl around my insides.

Reed.

"Where's Sela?" asked Jesse as he walked towards us through the cool sand. He'd also changed his clothing and now wore black lounge pants and a matching hooded sweatshirt.

Reed sighed. "She has a migraine."

"You know, I hate to be the one to break it to you," said Jesse, "but, your fiancée is an irritating bitch."

He stuck his hands in his pockets and chuckled. "She definitely has her moments."

64

I stared at Reed as he stood there looking towards the ocean and felt envious of Sela. With his eyes glittering in the moonlight and his hair blowing in the wind, he looked like a model, posing for a picture. If I were Sela and hadn't seen him for a while, he wouldn't have been out here with us. I would have tied him to the bed and had my way, several times over by now.

Of course, I'd never had a migraine so I shouldn't judge.

Feeling a little loose-lipped because of the wine, I cleared my throat. "Would you like to join us? There's plenty of wine."

He turned and smiled. "No, thank you. I just wanted to let you know that I hadn't forgotten about you two."

"You're not going skinny-dipping with us?" asked Jesse.

"No, I'll give you lovebirds some privacy," he said, his mouth twitching.

Jesse stood up. "Nonsense, we don't need privacy, big brother. We didn't come here for sex."

"Well, although I'd love to join you," he said, "I have to get back to Sela before she wakes up mom and dad. If she thinks I went skinny-dipping without her, she'll blow a gasket."

"You'd better go back then," I said. "We're not staying out here much longer, anyway."

Plus, there was no way I could drop my clothes when he was watching. At least not here on the beach.

"Well, you two have fun," he said, turning to go back. "Don't do anything I wouldn't do."

"Good luck with the shrew!" hollered Jesse.

Reed raised his hand but didn't look back.

***

Michael

I watched them frolicking in the water after the other man left. They couldn't see me hiding between the rocks, but my view was clear, especially of *her*.

It was the perfect night. The moon was full and the setting was made for lovers.

It was made for us.

When Sinclair stepped out of the water, she looked almost naked in her pale wet panties and bra. Her curves set me on fire and my hand moved inside of my trousers, watching her as I pumped my cock. I wanted nothing more than to lick the salt from her breasts as I thrust in and out of her wetness while she whispered my name, begging me for more. These thoughts consumed me and soon I shuddered into my fist, imagining the satisfaction in her eyes when it was over, as we held each other close and spoke of our future.

Soon, my love.

Chapter Eight

Reed

I walked back towards the house, wondering why the hell I hadn't just said *fuck it*, and stayed with Jesse and Sinclair. Not only would it have been interesting to see how far they'd go with their little farce, but the thought of getting a glimpse of Sinclair's body naked, well, it was enough to make me strain in my pants. As far as I was concerned, I could still appreciate a beautiful woman without touching her.

Unlike my father.

Sighing, I walked into the house and up to the guestroom to check on Sela. It was dark and empty.

Fuck.

I left and began searching the house for her as quietly as I could so I wouldn't wake up George, Gretchen, or my parents. When I finally made it to the library, I stopped in my tracks. Sela was sitting on the sofa, wearing a flimsy pink robe, and drinking a glass of champagne with Jack. As soon as he noticed me, Jack stood up and moved behind the sofa.

I forced a smile. "What's going on in here?"

"What does it look like?" asked Sela, a little gleam in her eyes.

Jack smiled and patted the sofa cushion. "Son, sit down."

"No thanks. So I see your migraine went away."

67

"Yes, after my bath. I went out to look for you and bumped into your father," said Sela, running a hand through the back of her damp hair. "We've been chatting."

"Is that so?" I asked.

Jack cleared his throat. "Yes. We haven't had much of a chance to talk yet. So we decided to have a quick glass of champagne to celebrate your upcoming wedding and talk about you."

"Oh, did my father reminisce about my childhood?" I asked, knowing very well that he wasn't around enough to know much about it. Nor did he really care, since I wasn't his biological child and he was a prick.

"No, but we did talk about *acting*, actually," said Sela. "Your father seems to think I might have a future career in Hollywood."

I looked at Jack, who nodded. "Yes, she expressed an interest in it and I told her I might be able to help."

I turned back to Sela. "So, what about modeling?"

She shrugged. "Well, I can do both."

"You're already complaining about how busy you are. I don't see how you can," I said.

"Listen," said Jack, looking down at his watch. "I think I'll head up to bed so you two can discuss this in private. It's getting late."

I folded my arms across my chest. "Good idea. I'm sure mom's probably wondering where you are."

He stared at me for a minute and then nodded.

68

"Goodnight, Mr. Eddington," said Sela, standing up. She walked over and threw her arms around him. "Thanks *so* much for the advice."

"Um, well, yes," he said, patting her on the back.

"Goodnight, Jack," I said, as she released him and he began walking towards the door.

He turned and paused at the door. "Goodnight, Reed."

I looked down and frowned. "You might want to zip up. Your fly is down."

Jack's eyes flashed to Sela and the guilt on his face was enough to send me to prison for manslaughter. Amazingly enough, however, I kept my cool. I wanted to break his fucking neck, but a larger part of me wanted to believe that even *he* wouldn't stoop that low.

"What were you doing in here with him, Sela?" I asked her after he slipped out the door.

Sela stood up. "What do you mean?" she asked, not quite meeting my eyes.

I moved closer to her. "His pants were unzipped and you both looked a little suspicious."

"You're being ridiculous," snapped Sela. "Do you honestly think I'd do something like that? Seriously?"

I wasn't sure what lengths she would go for her career, but I was pretty certain she knew how powerful Jack was in Hollywood.

"I don't know. I really don't," I said, moving towards her. "But if you did..."

She stepped backwards and raised her chin. "What? You'd hurt me?"

I smiled, coldly. "No, but don't give me any ideas."

"Your threats, Reed, they are getting old."

I sighed wearily and rubbed my forehead. "Sela, I haven't threatened you, and frankly, I'm getting tired of your little escapades – first, *your* accusations, then the drugs, and now this... weirdness with Jack? I just don't get you."

She tightened her robe and started walking towards the door. "Believe whatever you want. I'm tired and going to bed."

"Do you need help finding *your* room?" I asked dryly.

She turned around and glared at me. "No but I'm sure you can find your old room, which is where you're obviously staying this weekend."

Then she stormed out of the library, and as far as I was concerned, possibly out of my future.

***

Sinclair

"Well, that was fun," I said dryly.

"Are you sure you're okay?" asked Jesse. "Is your foot still bleeding?"

I stopped walking for a second and removed my flip-flop. "A little. The cut isn't too bad."

"We should have stayed in the water then," he said.

"Hell no," I said. "What if a shark would have smelled the blood and came looking for me?"

"Oh, you worry too much," he said.

"You don't worry enough," I retorted.

It was shortly after one o'clock in the morning and we were walking back towards the house.

Well, I was limping.

After getting the courage to strip down to my underwear, I'd finally found myself in the ocean with Jesse, who'd, thankfully, kept his shorts on. After going out just past my chest, I'd stepped on something sharp. When I swam back to shore, I'd noticed that my foot was bleeding.

"I just hope I don't get any blood on your mom's carpeting."

"You'll be fine," he said.

When we got to the house, I talked Jesse into carrying me back to my room.

"Jesus," he wheezed, carrying me up the stairs. "Maybe you *should* cut back on the carbs."

I squeezed his bicep. "Maybe you should start working on building these puny muscles."

"Cruel, Sin, cruel," he said in a strained voice.

When we finally reached my room, he dropped me onto the bed. "I think... I'm going... to die," he gasped, bending down to catch his breath.

"Oh, you'll be fine. Could you start my bathwater? I asked, examining my foot. The cut was pretty minor. "And see if there are any Band-Aids in the bathroom?"

He stood up straight. "God, you'd think we were married or something."

"Hey, you're the one who wanted to pretend we were a couple."

"Yeah, yeah, yeah," he said, walking towards the bathroom.

A minute later, he walked out of the bathroom carrying three Band-Aids and looking confused. "For some reason, the water isn't working," he said.

I groaned. "Seriously?"

"The pipes are making a weird noise but nothing is coming out. Obviously, you can't take a shower or bath in there."

"Crap. I need to take a shower or *something*. I'm all salty from the ocean."

"Try mine. I'm right down the hallway – the last door. You can use it while I go and have a snack downstairs. I'm freakin' starving."

"Well, okay."

"Here," said Jesse, handing me the Band-Aids. "This should take care of the blood, although, it looks like you may have stopped bleeding already."

I put all three bandages on, just in case. I wasn't about to piss Mimi off. "Thanks, Jesse."

"No problem. Do you want me to scrounge you up a snack, too?"

"No, thanks."

"I was only kidding," he said, kissing the top of my head. "You're not fat at all. If you want to eat, don't hold back."

"No, I'm fine."

"Okay. Go take your shower then, hopefully *my* shower is working."

"I hope so."

"Well, let me know if it isn't."

"Oh, I will."

He smiled. "Okay, I'll see you, later."

"Thanks."

After he left, I grabbed my robe, shampoo, and shower gel. Then I went in search of his room.

***

Reed

After Sela left, I raided the liquor cabinet in the library. With a satisfied grin, I grabbed a bottle of Jack's most expensive tequila, sat down on the couch, and proceeded to get drunk.

It didn't take long.

Less than an hour later, I staggered back to my bedroom. When I closed the door, I was surprised to hear the water running in the bathroom.

Sela?

I walked over to my bathroom and slowly pushed the door open. Sure enough, I could see flashes of her naked body through the clouded glass shower door.

Fuck it.

Although I was still pissed, I was also drunk and hornier than shit.

I slipped off my clothes and opened up the shower door, determined to have *my* way with Sela. She was still *my* fiancée, after all.

"Oh, my God!" she screamed.

I blinked in confusion. The vision standing before me wasn't Sela. This one had glistening soft curves, cat-like green eyes, and long, dark hair that reached her lower back.

I was so hard, it was almost painful.

"Reed!" gasped Sinclair, turning away so that all I could see was the water dripping down her heart-shaped ass.

"Shit... I'm sorry," I said, closing the door, instantly sobering up.

I picked up my clothes and quickly left the bathroom.

Sinclair

Oh, my God.
Had that just happened?

My heart was still racing as I hurried to wash off the rest of the soap from my body. I tried pushing away the image of him staring at me in the shower, the desire in his eyes.

I couldn't help but smile. He had definitely liked what he'd seen.

And, oh, hot damn, that body of his! Standing in all of his naked glory – the smooth chiseled chest, hard biceps, and that thick piece of manhood between his legs, pointing right at me! He was ready to go and I freakin' scared him off!

Engaged, I reminded myself.

I hit the shower wall and turned the cold water up, wondering if it worked for women, too.

Chapter Nine

Reed

I waited for Sinclair to finish, still confused as to why she was in *my* bedroom, using *my* shower. If she wouldn't have looked so horrified, I would have thought she'd planned some kind of seduction. Although I'd like to say her plan wouldn't have worked, I still couldn't get the image of her hot, naked body out of my mind.

Jesus, I needed to sober up.

When she finally stepped out of the bathroom, she was wearing a short blue terrycloth robe and holding her things in front of her, like a shield.

I smiled sheepishly. "Well, that was awkward."

Her cheeks grew pink and she nodded. "Very."

"I guess I should ask – why are you using my shower?"

Her eyebrows shot up. *"Your* shower?"

"Yes. This is my bedroom, my shower."

"I thought it was Jesse's."

"His is across the hall."

"Oh, I'm so sorry," she said, looking mortified.

I rubbed the back of my neck. "Don't worry about it. We'll just pretend it didn't happen."

And that I didn't see those sinfully, delicious curves hidden under that robe.

"Okay."

"You'd better get out of here before Jesse comes looking for you. He might get jealous," I said, biting back a smile.

"Right."

"Sweet dreams," I said, lying back against my pillows, my arms behind my neck.

Blushing, she nodded. "Um, sweet dreams."

I watched as she left, hoping that my dreams would include me joining her in the shower.

***

Sinclair

I left Reed's bedroom, my face still burning at the memory of seeing him naked. As I moved down the hallway to my room, thinking of all the wicked things I wanted to do with that body, I ran into Jesse, who was just coming from the kitchen.

"Oh good, you're done with your shower," he whispered. "Did you find everything okay?"

I told him what had happened and he had to actually cover his mouth as he began laughing hysterically. "Stop, it wasn't funny," I whispered.

"Oh, my God, are you kidding me? That's hilarious."

"It was mortifying."

He wiggled his eyebrows. "So, was he happy to see you?"

"You mean aroused?"

"Yes. Was he *sprung*?"

"I didn't even look," I managed to say with a straight face.

"Bullshit."

I smiled. "Okay, I guess he wasn't totally turned off by seeing me naked."

Jesse bit his lower lip and got this faraway look in his eyes. "You know... I wonder if you could somehow seduce Reed. That would take care of the Sela problem."

I stared at him in surprise. "No, absolutely not."

He studied me for a minute and then smiled. "Okay. Forget I mentioned it."

From the look in his eyes, however, I knew he was still mulling the idea over in his mind.

"I mean it," I warned. "I would never do something like that. He's engaged and I'm not going to come between that."

"I totally understand. Listen, don't forget we're going shopping for your dress tomorrow. So, get some sleep."

"Okay. I have to cut Reed's hair in the morning first."

"Right after that then," he said.

"Okay, goodnight."

"Goodnight, Sin."

I stepped to my bedroom door and glanced back to find Jesse still looking at me.

"What?" I asked.

"Nothing," he said, turning away. "Sleep well."

"You too," I answered, knowing I'd probably sleep like an angel but dream like the Devil, if the images of Reed didn't leave my sinful mind.

Chapter Ten

Reed.

I'd fallen asleep alone but woke up with someone's lips wrapped around my cock.

"Jesus," I gasped, as her warm, wet mouth moved up and down.

"Good morning," whispered Sela. "Miss me?"

I couldn't even answer – she had me, quite literally, by the balls. I closed my eyes and let her keep doing what she did best – fucking with me. As her mouth moved faster and I went deeper, an image of Sinclair, dripping wet in the shower, consumed me. I imagined it was her hands touching me, her mouth drawing me in, and I exploded.

"Wow," smiled Sela, sitting up. "That was quick. I guess you missed me last night."

"I guess," I answered, closing my eyes again.

When I was able to catch my bearings, I opened my eyes and studied Sela. The scene with Jack in the library *really* fucking disturbed me. I would have hoped that I could trust her – she was my fiancée. But the guilt in Jack's eyes kept haunting me. Sela had already hidden the drugs from me; what else was she really capable of?

"Tell me something, do you love me?" I asked.

She frowned. "Do I love you? What kind of question is that?"

"A pretty easy one. Do you, Sela?"

She stood up, walked over to the mirror, and ran her fingers through her hair. "You make me happy. Isn't that enough?"

"I make you happy? It doesn't seem like it."

Our eyes met in the mirror's reflection. "Well, you do, Reed." She turned around smiled. "Very. That's why we're perfect for each other. Happiness and amazing sex."

"But not love?"

She waved her hand. "Oh, come on, only fools believe in love," she said. "As far as I'm concerned, people confuse lust with love. Love is a fantasy, not a reality."

"So, what you're really saying is that you're not in love with me?"

She laughed. "Reed, admit it, you're not in love with me either! But, you have to admit, we *are* good together."

She was right. I guess I wasn't really in love with her. The sex was good and we had fun together. Definite chemistry, but was *that* enough to spend the rest of my life with someone? It obviously worked for Jack, but he was an asshole.

I got out of bed. "I'm going to take a shower."

She smiled coyly. "Would you like me to join you?"

"No time. Have too much to do this morning," I said, heading towards the bathroom.

"What am I supposed to do?" she pouted.

I glanced back at her. "Relax for a change. Lay out by the pool or go for a swim at the beach."

She raised her eyebrows. "Alone?"

I shrugged. "Maybe Sinclair will join you after she cuts my hair."

Sela scowled. "I don't like her."

"Why?"

She raised her chin. "I just don't."

I sighed. "Well, then I guess you're on your own until this afternoon."

"Fine," she said, "but after you're finished with everything, you *owe* me."

"You'll have my full attention, I promise."

She pulled her robe in tighter and walked towards the door. "I can't believe you're letting that girl touch your hair."

"I'm sure she'll do a good job."

Staring at me intently, she asked, "I wonder what your brother sees in her?"

Sinclair?

She was beautiful, witty, and sexier than hell. In fact, even now I was having a problem getting her out of my mind. But Jesse, what did my brother see in her?

"I don't know what he sees in her," I answered honestly. Sinclair definitely wasn't his type. Not by a long shot.

Pleased with that answer, Sela nodded and left the room.

***

Sinclair

I woke up around nine o'clock and noticed that the water was now working fine in the shower.

"Of course," I grumbled out loud.

I took a quick one and then slipped on a pair of white shorts and a bright coral tank-top. As I was putting my hair up into a ponytail, there was a knock on my door.

"Hey, girlfriend," smiled Jesse under his favorite Maui Jim sunglasses.

"Hey, sunshine," I said, staring at his hot pink polo shirt and white chinos.

"Hungry?" asked Jesse, pushing the glasses above his head.

"A little."

"Let's go downstairs. Gretchen usually has breakfast put away by now, but I bet we can scrape something up in the kitchen."

I yawned. "What about coffee?"

"Well, that's available all day long, silly girl."

I slipped on a pair of strapless white sandals and followed Jesse to the kitchen where we found Reed, reading the paper and drinking coffee at the counter.

"Hi," he said, putting the newspaper down. "Was wondering when you guys were going to wake up."

Jesse put his arm around my shoulders and smiled. "Sin was feeling frisky this morning."

Reed grinned. "Is that so?"

"Oh yeah. This girl is insatiable," answered Jesse, turning on the coffee machine. "I'm going to be sore all day."

I elbowed him in the ribs. "You should talk – I'm the one walking funny."

Reed's eyes landed on my crotch, triggering an immediate surge of heat. He looked away quickly, and grabbed his cup.

"Um, so, are you ready for your haircut?" I asked.

"Yes, if you are," he answered, finishing the last of his coffee.

"My scissors are in my suitcase. Where should we do it?"

"How about your bedroom? Maybe on the balcony?"

"Sure," I said as Jesse handed me a cup of coffee.

"Even though I'd *love* to watch Sin do you on the balcony, I'm going to stick around here and eat some breakfast," said Jesse.

I turned back to look at Jesse, who had a big shit-eating grin on his face.

"Stop," I mouthed.

His eyes widened, innocently. "What?"

Reed stood up, looking yummy in a tight white concert tee that not only emphasized his tan, but endless broad shoulders and a narrow waist. As he turned to rinse out the coffee cup, I quickly checked out his butt in the low-riding faded blue jeans and despised Sela more than ever.

He turned back around and his lips curved up on the one side. "So, to your bedroom?"

"Ah, yeah."

"I'll follow you," he said, walking towards me.

We left the kitchen and walked up the stairs, me leading the way. For some reason I was very conscious of how my own butt looked and had an urge to glance back to see where exactly his eyes were. Of course, I chickened out and just kept going up.

When we entered my bedroom, I grabbed my makeup bag and pulled out the scissors. "So, just a trim then?"

He opened up the patio door. "Sure, sounds great," he said.

I followed him outside to a tall metal bistro table. He sat down and looked at me, his expression unreadable.

I bit the side of my lip. "We should really wet your hair first."

"Should I take another shower?"

Flashes of him naked and happy to see me made my nipples tighten in my bra. "I... um... how about wetting your hair in the sink? That would be so much easier."

"Sure."

I followed him into the bathroom.

"I'd better remove the shirt," he said. "So it doesn't get wet."

Oh, my God... yes!

"Good idea," I answered in a surprisingly professional tone.

Then, in what seemed like slow motion, Reed tugged his shirt out of his jeans, raised it over his rock-hard abs, and lifted it over his broad shoulders while I watched – my mouth physically unable to close.

Looking in the mirror, he quickly ran a hand through his hair, then turned back to me and held out his shirt.

I stared at him in confusion.

"Can you take this?" he asked, his mouth twitching.

"Oh, yes," I answered, flushed and breathless.

As I hung it on a hook behind the door, I could smell a trace of his cologne and had to fight the urge to bring the shirt to my nose to inhale the wonderful scent.

God, I was so pathetic.

I turned around to find him staring at me in amusement, as if he could somehow read my mind.

"Ready?" he asked, leaning back against the sink with his arms crossed.

I managed a smile. "Yeah."

I tried to appear unaffected by him, but it wasn't easy; not when I hadn't had sex in so long and was this close to a half-naked man.

And not just any half-naked man.

This one was so effin' hot, he could raise a girl's temperature in the next state.

"What do you think?" he asked.

Oh, my God... what did I think?

His chest was perfectly chiseled and his abs, obviously, the result of countless crunches.

And that was just what was above his jeans!

After witnessing what was hiding underneath last night, I was having trouble concentrating on much more. Without a doubt, I knew I was definitely in the danger zone with Reed. In fact, if he even *hinted* at sex, I'd probably drag *him* by his hair into my bedroom and make sure both of us were sore for the next couple of days.

Sensing my fugue, he repeated the question.

"What... what do you mean?" I asked.

"What do you think I should do? Put my head in the tub or in the sink?"

"Oh," I blushed, thinking of another place he could put his head. "The sink should be fine. If you won't be too uncomfortable?"

"It should be fine," he said, turning around. He turned on the water and then bent his head down near the faucet, giving me a great view of his wide, muscular back. I imagined my hands exploring those hard planes and felt a fluttery tingle between my legs.

"Sinclair, ready?"

Jesus, get a grip, Sinclair.

"Yes, sorry," I said.

My hands were trembling slightly as I bent over him and slid my fingers into his soft, brown hair. I exhaled slowly, knowing at that moment, I'd never wanted to touch anyone's head as much as this man's.

"That feels good," he murmured, as I ran my fingers through the wet strands and began massaging his scalp.

"We usually massage the head before every cut to relax our customers in the shop," I said, my voice slightly hitched.

"Is that right?" he asked.

"Yeah."

"You okay?"

"I'm fine. Are you okay?" I managed to say, wondering which was wetter at the moment, me or his hair.

"I'm great. In fact, you can massage my head anytime," he answered, a smile in his voice.

I didn't trust myself to answer. Instead, I turned off the water and began patting his hair with a towel. "You ready?" I asked, clearing my throat.

He stood up and looked down into my eyes. "I am, are you?"

I swallowed. "Um, sure, let's go back outside."

His eyes lowered and his tongue licked the side of his upper lip. "Looks like I got you wet," he said softly.

My eyes widened. "What?"

He raised his fingertips and touched a spot right above my breasts. "Water."

I looked down and smiled sheepishly. The fact of the matter was the entire front of my entire tank was pretty damp. "It's okay, I'm used to it."

He grinned and motioned towards the doorway. "After you."

I cleared my throat and proceeded to walk back out to the balcony. When he sat down, I picked up my comb and scissors.

"How did you sleep last night?" he asked as I began combing his hair.

"Okay," I said, trying to avoid his icy stare. "You?"

"Actually, I had a hard time sleeping."

"Oh?"

"I thought since I'd had a few shots of tequila, I'd sleep like a baby. But, no such luck."

"Hmm..." I said, not knowing that he'd been drinking. Maybe there was a chance he'd forgotten our little encounter?

"Fact is, I only got a few hours of sleep."

I leaned over him to grab my scissors, the side of my breast brushing his shoulder. "Sorry," I said.

"I'm not complaining," he said, his voice low.

Our eyes met briefly and my mouth went dry.

"I'll be right back," I said, stepping backwards. "I need my other comb."

And to break this freakin' sexual tension for a few seconds.

***

Reed

"Okay," I said and then nonchalantly put my hand over my jeans to cover up my half-cocked hard-on. Ever since she'd started undressing me with her eyes and massaging my head, I hadn't been able to think straight.

"What's Sela doing today?" she asked, returning a little while later.

"Relaxing."

She began combing my hair again. "So, when's the big wedding?"

I sighed, feeling my hard-on begin to recede. "We don't have a date set yet."

She leaned in front of me, giving me a partial view of her cleavage.

"How short do you want it?" she asked.

"I'll let you decide."

She studied my hair intently. "Okay, I think I'll just take a little off."

"I'm yours, do whatever you want," I said, knowing I was playing with fire. I knew it was wrong but I couldn't help myself.

Her cheeks turned pink and I wondered what was going through that beautiful skull of hers. I hadn't planned on flirting with her at all, but the electricity between us was staggering. I was no longer thinking with a clear head, just a stiff one.

"So, you and Jesse are pretty serious, huh?" I asked after a few minutes of silence.

She shrugged. "We're just having fun right now."

"I see. You know, he never really dated much when he lived here."

"Is that right?"

"Fact is – I could have *sworn* that he was gay."

Her hands paused. "Really?"

"But, now that I've met you, there's no doubt in my mind that he's straight. Or," I smiled, "if he was gay, you must have certainly converted him."

She chuckled. "I doubt I could convert Jesse into anything."

"Believe me, if anyone could convert a gay man, it would be you."

Sinclair stepped back and looked at me, her full lips forming into an amused grin. "Are you flirting with me?"

"Who me? I'm just telling it like it is. You're a beautiful girl."

"Well, thank you," she said, raising the scissors again. "Sela is also very beautiful."

"Yes, she is."

She frowned. "She doesn't seem to like me very much."

"Don't take it personally. Sela feels threatened by most other women, one way or the other."

"That's too bad. She seems to have everything – beauty, a successful career, a nice guy."

I cocked an eyebrow. "You think I'm nice?"

"Aren't you?'

"If it gets me what I want," I teased. "Otherwise I'm a real prick."

She smiled. "Oh, really?'

"Why do you think I'm being so nice to you? Obviously I wanted something."

She stopped cutting and took a step back. "I... um..."

I chuckled, enjoying the way I kept making her cheeks turn pink. "A haircut."

She smirked. "Well, I guess being nice *does* pay off."

"So, what are your plans until the party?" I asked as she concentrated intently on the front of my hair.

"We're doing a little shopping and then I'm not really sure," she said.

My cell phone started chirping and she stopped cutting.

"Don't worry about it," I said. "It can wait."

"Oh, okay."

"So, tell me a little about yourself," I said, as she resumed cutting. "Where are you from?"

"Well, I grew up in Stanton, that's where my parents still live."

"Are your parents normal or fucked up like mine?"

She laughed. "Fucked up?"

"I guess Jesse didn't tell you?"

"Well, he mentioned they were difficult."

"That's an understatement."

"Well, they've been pleasant to me, so far."

"Good. Just be careful around Jack."

"Why?"

"Let's just say, he doesn't always remember he's married."

"Oh. That's not cool."

"No, it isn't."

"Poor Mimi."

I stared out towards the ocean, thinking about how many times I'd wanted to pound the shit out of Jack. Once, when I was in my early twenties, I almost did. Unfortunately, Mimi treated *me* like the asshole that night. She had stepped between us and had actually told me to mind my own business. "She's known for years but..."

"Lives with it."

"Unfortunately."

She was silent for a while and then said, "I had a 'Jack' in my life once. One time was more than enough for me."

"He cheated on you?"

She looked me in the eyes. "Yeah, and it hurts like bloody hell. That's why I'm not going to give my heart away again, not that easily."

The message was clear and I started feeling like an asshole. Although my current situation was complicated, I was still engaged and had no right to flirt with her. Not until I got my shit together and figured out what I really wanted.

But, it wasn't easy, every time I looked into those pools of green, I was captivated.

"I don't blame you. Giving yourself to someone should never be done lightly," I said.

So, what in the hell was I doing with Sela?

"I'm not in a hurry anyway."

"So, I take it Jesse isn't *the* one?"

She gave me a lopsided grin. "Like I said, we're just having fun."

"How old are you?" I asked.

"Twenty-four."

"Well, there you go, you have plenty of time."

"That's what I keep telling myself."

My phone started chirping again.

"You should probably answer that," she said, bending down to clean up some of the hair on the ground. "I'm finished, anyway."

I ran a hand across my head. "Okay, thanks."

She smiled up at me. "Don't thank me until you've looked in the mirror."

"I'm sure it looks great," I said, standing up. I walked into the bedroom and looked at my reflection in the dresser mirror.

"What do you think?" she asked, coming up behind me.

I ran my hands through it and nodded. "It looks awesome. Just like I knew it would."

"Good," she beamed.

I turned to her. "So, what do I owe you?"

She looked up at me and shook her head. "Nothing. Nothing at all."

I stared down into her sparkling green eyes and swallowed hard. Why was she having such an effect on me? I was used to women flirting, even throwing themselves at me, and had no problem resisting.

But this girl?

Fuck, I wanted to pull her into my arms, taste those beautiful lips. But I knew it was wrong and she'd be completely horrified.

Sighing, I said. "How about I offer you my services?"

Her eyes widened. "Your services?"

"You ever need any legal advice," I said, pulling out my wallet. "Call me. Here's my card."

She nodded. "Okay, thanks. Although, no offense, I hope I never have to use this."

I chuckled and slipped my T-shirt back over my head. "None taken. Maybe we could just have lunch sometime?"

Sinclair smiled. "If I ever make it out to New York, I'll look you up."

"Good."

My phone chirped again and I pulled it out of my pocket.

Sela.

"Well, thanks again for the cut," I said, walking towards the door. Sela was going to be pissed that I hadn't answered her calls, although, she hadn't left me a message either. It couldn't have been that important.

"No problem. I suppose I should go find Jesse," she said behind me.

I turned to look at her one last time and my eyes were instantly rewarded. The ceiling fan was obviously having an effect on Sinclair's nipples, because they were poking through the front of her tank-top, which was still slightly damp. I wondered what shade of pink they were and the head of my cock began pulsating in my jeans.

Jesus.

"See you later," I said in a husky voice.

She reached up and lightly brushed a piece of hair from my cheek. "There, that's better," she murmured.

There it was again, that look in her sexy green eyes. Like she was dying of thirst and I was the last bottle of Fiji on the face of the earth. Or maybe *I* was the one dying and *she* was the last bottle of ice-cold beer.

She licked her lips, and before I could stop myself, I decided to live.

Chapter Eleven

Sinclair

When his lips captured mine, I moaned and slid my arms around his neck, pulling him closer. His mouth was hot and demanding and when our tongues met, my legs turned to jelly.

His hands went around my waist and then down to my ass, pulling me against his pelvis. When I felt Reed's excitement poking me through his jeans, I had an incredible urge to tear them off and climb aboard, I wanted him so bad. Instead, I reached one of my hands down and rubbed the outside of his zipper, relishing in the hard maleness of him straining to get out.

He groaned against my mouth and slid his fingers around the curve of my ass, then down the crevice until he was lightly touching the junction between my legs through my shorts. I almost came right then and there as I gasped in pleasure.

Holy hell, did I want this guy.

As his other hand reached up and touched my breast, I pushed him away.

"Reed," I said, breathless. "You're engaged!"

He stepped back and ran a hand over his face. "I know, fuck... I'm sorry."

"You'd better leave," I said, adjusting my shorts.

He nodded. "I'm sorry. I..."

"Let's just forget this happened," I said, forcing a smile.

He stared at me like he had more to say but just couldn't find the words. If he didn't leave now, however, I knew that neither of us would be talking.

I lowered my eyes. "Reed, just please... leave."

"Okay," he replied, turning away.

I closed the door behind him and leaned against it, wondering what the hell had just happened. Obviously, it was wrong, but that didn't stop me from wanting more of it.

You're not messing up someone's relationship, I told myself. *Who cares if his fiancée is a royal bitch – nobody deserves to get cheated on.*

Sighing, I changed my clothes and went to go find Jesse.

***

Reed

After that scene with Sinclair, I knew there was no way that I was ready for marriage. I decided that after the anniversary party, I would lock up all my breakables and talk to Sela. For now, however, I decided it would be best to stay away from Sinclair and be a little more attentive towards Sela.

I owed her that.

With a sense of relief, I went in search of Sela and found her in a miniscule pink bikini, lounging next to the outdoor pool.

"Where have you been?" she asked frigidly.

"Can't you tell?" I asked, spreading my arms apart and turning around.

She wrinkled her nose. "Is that *her* idea of a haircut?"

"What's wrong with it?" I asked, knowing perfectly well that the only thing wrong was the fact that Sinclair had given it to me.

"It's fine," she said. "If *you* like it, that's all that matters."

I frowned. "It's a good, solid trim and it looks the same as it usually does when I have it done. In fact," I said, running a hand through my hair. "I think she did a better job than my last stylist."

She stretched her arms, pushing out her breasts. "It's fine," she said. "I'll still let you in my bed."

I grinned. "You will, huh?"

"Oh, look," she said, looking beyond me. "Jack's coming to join us."

I turned to see him closing the patio door, wearing a white robe and holding, what appeared to be, a large Bloody Mary.

"Hey, kids," he said, smiling, brightly as he moved towards us.

"Jack," I said.

"Good morning," said Sela. "Oh, that looks *so* refreshing," she said, motioning towards his cocktail.

He stopped and stared down at Sela. "You want it? I can have Gretchen whip up another one. I told her to keep them coming anyway."

Sela removed her sunglasses and batted her lashes. "Oh, I couldn't take *yours*."

"Of course you could, my dear," he said, handing it to her. "I insist."

"Oh, thank you, Mr. Eddington," she gushed, acting like a flirty little schoolgirl.

Jack smiled. "You're practically my daughter now," he said. "*Our* house is your house."

"Oh, thanks, 'daddy'," she giggled.

"See, I like the sound of that already," he said, running a finger over his mustache.

"So," I interrupted, feeling a little pissed off at the way the asshole was gawking at Sela's body. "Get a good night's sleep, Jack?"

He removed his robe, revealing skinny limbs and a fleshy belly. "Marvelous," he said, rubbing his hands together. "In fact, I'm so refreshed that I've decided to do some laps in the pool this morning, before they start preparing the house for tonight's party."

"Good idea," I said.

He swung his arms around, stretching them out, and then dove into the deep end of the water.

I turned to Sela. "So, I'll be back in a couple of hours," I said. "I have some errands to run. Unless, you'd like to tag along?"

She took a sip of her drink and then set it down next to her. "No, I think I'll just hang out at the pool for a few hours," she said, pulling at her bikini bottoms. "Work on this tan."

"Okay, call me if you need anything," I said, bending down and kissing her on the cheek.

"Okay," she said, grabbing her tanning oil, "could you do me a favor and put some of this on my back first?"

"Sure."

She turned over onto her stomach and untied her bikini top.

I poured some oil into my palms and proceeded to rub it over her shoulders and down her back. As she sighed in approval, I thought of Sinclair, wishing it was her skin that I was running my hands over.

"If you'd like to continue this inside," purred Sela, "I'll let you oil my front, too."

I stood up and chuckled. "Wish I could, but I need to pick up Jack and Mimi's gift."

"Okay. Maybe later?"

"If there's time," I said, looking at my watch.

"If there's time?" she repeated, raising her eyebrows.

"Don't worry," I said, sensing a tantrum brewing. "I'm sure there will be."

"Hurry back then," she said, grabbing her iPod.

I glanced towards Jack, who was still engrossed in his laps, then walked back towards the house, wondering which was more unsettling – leaving Sela alone with Jack, or my new obsession with Sinclair.

Chapter Twelve

Sinclair

"That's the one," nodded Jesse, a look of approval on his face. "That dress is sinful, it's over-the-top, and it fucking *rocks*. In fact, I think it could end some perfectly stable marriages."

I turned towards him and pulled at the front. "You don't think it's too revealing?"

He glanced at my very exposed cleavage. "Oh, no... you'll be overdressed to some people's standards at tonight's soiree. Remember, there will be musicians, actors, and more skanky, anorexic models."

I stared at myself in the mirror at this swanky, upscale dress store called Dolce's. The average outfit cost well over one thousand dollars and the red chiffon gown I currently had on was triple that price. I had to admit, however, I liked how it hugged my body and the way my leg peeked out from the slit on the side.

"You sure you want to pay this much?" I asked, looking at the tag again.

He stood up and put his arm around me. "Yes, sweetie," he whispered in my ear. "I only ask that you let me borrow it from you, someday."

My eyebrows shot up.

He put his hands on his hips. "Don't look at me like that, Sin. You know I'd rock that dress."

"I'm sure, but... I never knew you..."

He smiled, wickedly. "Oh there are many things you don't know, sweetheart."

I giggled. "Oh, you are wild and dirty, aren't you?"

He let out a playful growl. "You have no freakin' idea."

***

We purchased the dress along with a pair of sexy black heels and then went out for lunch at a cozy restaurant along Huntington Beach.

"So, what do you think of my family so far?" asked Jesse after finishing a peanut-butter-and-banana-Panini sandwich.

"Well, your mom is definitely old fashioned and set in her ways," I said. "Which I can see why you wouldn't want to tell her you're gay."

He laughed. "Could you imagine? She'd lock herself in her room with a bottle of valium and never come out."

I chuckled. "Definitely. But what about your dad? I mean, he must work with a lot of gay people. I'm sure he'd be much more understanding."

Jesse sighed. "You'd think, huh? The fact is that I've heard him bash gays, minorities, and women with small breasts. He's a total dickhead, and frankly, I'm ashamed he's blood-related."

"That's too bad," I said.

"Not only that, he's cheated on my mother more times than I can count. She's a prude and annoying as hell most of the time, but she doesn't deserve to get shit on by him."

"I heard about that," I said, taking a last bite of my salad. "It's a shame."

"Reed told you?"

I nodded and took a sip of my Chardonnay. "It's too bad. Why doesn't she just leave him?"

"That is the question, isn't it?" interrupted a deep voice behind me.

"What – did Sela let you out of your cage?" laughed Jesse.

He smirked. "No, she forgot to lock it."

"Sit down," said Jesse. "Join us."

Reed sat down next to me. When his leg brushed mine, my skin felt like it was on fire.

"Thanks. I saw your car outside as I was driving back to the house," he said. "I hope I'm not interrupting anything?"

"No, not at all," said Jesse, pulling out his ringing phone. He looked at it and then at me. "It's Alex. Please excuse me for a minute. I'm going to take this outside."

"Sure," I said.

The waitress showed up just as Jesse walked away. Reed ordered a beer and a bacon cheeseburger with fries and then moved across from me.

"What, do I smell funny?" I joked.

He grinned. "Not at all. I just don't trust myself sitting close to you."

I blushed and took another sip of wine.

"Hey," he said, reaching out to touch my hand. "I'm sorry about this morning. I mean, I am and I'm not."

I pulled my hand away from his. "You should be. What about Sela?"

He sat back and rubbed his chin. "You're right, it was shitty."

"Yes. Well, I'm really sorry, too," I said, looking out the window. "I should have pushed you away sooner."

"I'm hard to resist," he chuckled.

I shook my head and laughed. "Right…"

"Seriously, though," he said, "lets' just pretend that it never happened."

I nodded. "Sounds good to me."

"Sinclair, I just want you to know something, though," he said, looking into my eyes. "I'm not normally *that* guy."

"*That* guy?"

"The kind who fucks around. What happened back in your room, it wasn't right and it probably shouldn't have happened, but…"

I blinked, waiting for him to continue. "What?"

With a seductive curve of his lips he said, "It was pretty fucking amazing."

Hell yeah, and thinking about it made me squirmy. The way he was undressing me with his eyes didn't help matters, either.

"It was," I whispered.

We stared at each other in silence and then the waitress brought him his beer.

"So, excited about the party tonight?" I asked, trying to change the subject.

He smiled humorlessly. "Not really. I hate hobnobbing with the rich and famous. Most of them are so shallow and plastic."

Which sounded like his fiancée.

"Not your thing, huh?" I asked.

"Don't get me wrong, it's interesting to sit along the sidelines and watch the game when you're not a player."

"You're just a fan?"

"I'm more like the person dragged to the game and forced to watch. My parents know some pretty crazy people, and I have a feeling tonight is going to be nuts."

"Well, considering my life is pretty boring, I'm looking forward to a little craziness."

"That's a shame," he said, his eyes darkening. "I would think that Jesse would make it his mission to keep you from being bored. I know I would."

"He, um... he works a lot."

He drummed his knuckles on the table and sighed. "I'm also guilty as charged."

Out of the corner of my eye, I noticed Jesse coming towards us and relaxed. Reed made me nervous, tense, and incredibly horny. I still didn't quite trust myself around him, either. "Speak of the devil," I said.

"You okay?" asked Reed as Jesse sat down next to me.

"Just some problems at work," he said, glancing my way. From the serious look on his face, it was clear that Alex was being difficult.

"You don't have to check in at work this weekend, do you?" I asked.

He smiled, bitterly. "No, in fact, I think I may have just lost my job."

"Oh no," I said, grabbing his hand. "Are you serious?"

"Yeah."

His eyes filled with tears and my heart went out to him. I squeezed his hand. "It will be okay, Jesse. It will."

He looked away. "Right."

"Shit, you'll find a new job in no time," said Reed. "I have connections all over. I'm sure we can get you another position by the end of the week."

Jesse turned to me, his face distraught. "If you don't mind, I'd like to get back to the house to figure things out."

"Of course," I said, standing up. "Let's go."

He sighed. "No, um... could you stay with Reed? I really want to be alone right now," he said. "I might have to make a couple of calls anyway, and you don't want to hear what I have to say."

"Oh, okay," I said.

"Don't worry. I'll just bring Sinclair back to the house with me," said Reed, patting him on the shoulder. "You do what you've got to do."

"Appreciate it," he said, standing up. "I'll see you two back at the house." Then he left us without a backwards glance.

"Wow, he must have a lot invested in that job for him to be so upset."

"I think he's going to miss the benefits, more than anything," I said.

***

Michael

I watched them from the corner of the restaurant, and wondered why her gay friend had left and who, exactly, this other man was. Obviously, he couldn't be trusted around such a tempting creature and would have to be dealt with accordingly.

The waitress returned to my table and smiled. "Would you like another glass of wine?"

"No, thank you."

She hesitated, as if she had more to say.

I smiled up at her. "Yes?"

She sighed. "You may not remember me, but..."

I flashed her one of my most engaging smiles. Although I have met many people, I did not particularly recall this homely creature. "Of course I remember you," I lied. "How could I forget?"

She smiled back in pleasure. "It's been a long time. In fact, I think the last time I saw you, was at camp."

Ah, yes, now I remembered. She'd been just as annoying back then.

"Yes," I said. "That sounds about right."

She relaxed. "You look good."

"Thank you," I said. "So do you."

"Um, say... my shift is over now, would you like to join me for a drink? My treat?"

"Of course," I said, trying to hide my frustration.

She nodded and smiled, again. "Good, I'll be right back. Same thing?" she asked, pointing to my glass.

"Actually, why don't you bring me a cup of coffee? I have a large engagement that I need to attend to this evening."

"Wedding or funeral?" she asked.

"Anniversary party."

Chapter Thirteen

Reed

I thought Jesse's reaction to losing his job was a little emotional for a twenty-four-year-old man, gay or not. From the silent exchanges between Jesse and Sinclair, however, I realized that there was something more to it, but didn't dig. If my brother didn't want to divulge anything about his personal life to me, I certainly wasn't going to pry.

I'd expect the same from him.

"So, are you ready?" I asked Sinclair after finishing my lunch and second beer.

She grabbed her purse. "Yes. Do you want me to drive?"

I stopped abruptly, causing her to slam into me. "Excuse me?"

She steadied herself. "Are you too tipsy to drive?"

"First of all, I do not *get* 'tipsy'. I am either drunk or just plain sober."

"Which one are you?" she asked, her mouth twisting into one of those sexy grins I was beginning to crave.

Both, I thought, staring at her. As far as I was concerned, *she* made me feel inebriated. "I'm sober," I said. "Remember, I'm a lawyer. I know when to stop drinking before I get behind the wheel."

She laughed. "Right. So, I'm supposed to trust a lawyer?"

I put my hand on her back and guided her towards the door. "You watch too much television," I said, opening it, "which gives us all bad raps."

"Television, huh?" she said, as we walked out to the parking lot.

I raised the key fob and pointed it towards my car. "Of course," I said. "Not all of us are crooked. In fact, a lot of my cases are pro bono."

"Is this yours?" she asked, staring at the silver Mercedes SLS. "Pro bono seems to agree with you," she said.

I grinned. "This is just a rental."

She shook her head and got inside.

I slid into the driver's seat next to her and closed the door when the scent of Sinclair's perfume engulfed me. A light fruity fragrance, reminding me of the kiss we'd shared earlier. I tried to push the memory away, but her close proximity was making it difficult.

"Not quite a family car," she said, snapping on her seatbelt. "You and Sela are going to have to invest in a minivan."

"Nonsense," I smiled. "I'll have a special luggage rack installed. The kids will love the view from up there."

She threw her head back and laughed. It was a beautiful sound – feminine and purely genuine.

"Oh, my God, you're a hoot," she said.

I raised my eyebrows. "I'm a hoot?"

"Okay, you're kind of nuts – is that better?"

"Actually, you're the one who got into a car with me. *Now*, tell me who's nuts?" I said, giving her my most sinister grin.

"Touché."

"What kind of music do you like?" I asked, turning on the XM radio.

"Whatever you'd like," she said. "I'm easy."

"You're easy?"

She rolled her eyes. "God, you're a smartass, just like your brother. You know exactly what I mean."

"No, I don't. Please reiterate what it is you *exactly* mean, *Sin*."

She pointed at the road. "I'm about as *easy* as you are *hard-to-get*."

"Are you saying *I'm* easy?" I asked, feigning a look of shock.

She pulled her hair behind her ears and smiled. "Never met a guy who wasn't."

"I'm sure *you* haven't."

Her cheeks turned pink and I had an incredible urge to place them in my palms and feel their warmth. Instead, I found a song by *Adele* and settled with a few stolen glances of her profile as she stared off towards the ocean.

"Beautiful," I sighed.

Sinclair nodded. "Yes. It's incredible. Man, it must have been wonderful growing up in this area."

"I can't complain. My brother and I were very fortunate in many ways."

"So, what made you decide to move to New York?" she asked.

112

I shrugged. "My career. I was offered a partnership by an old friend three years ago and jumped on it. I guess I wanted a change at the time, and it seemed like the perfect opportunity."

She nodded. "I guess I can understand that. New York sounds fascinating."

"It is. You should come out and visit sometime, with Jesse."

"Maybe."

I turned up the music and we drove the rest of the way in silence while I cheated and took a much longer scenic route. When we finally reached the house, I was tempted to keep driving, just so I could enjoy her presence a little bit longer. She was definitely getting under my skin.

"So," I asked, as we pulled up to the house. "What do you usually do for fun when you're not working?"

She smiled. "For fun? Oh, I don't know – read, go for walks, hang out with friends."

"Jesse works that much, huh?" I asked, smiling.

She shrugged. "We go out when we can, but I usually have to be at the shop by six-thirty most mornings, so it's difficult."

"I hear that. When I'm not at the office, I'm at home, working."

"Wow, looks like they're already setting up for tonight," she said, motioning towards the party supply and catering trucks.

I looked at my watch, it was just after two-thirty. "I'm surprised my mother didn't have them here at sunrise. She lives for parties."

"I keep hearing that both of your parents are so boring and straight-laced. I guess I'm surprised to hear that their parties are wild and crazy. At least that's what Jesse says."

I nodded. "Jack's in showbiz. Having outrageous parties is kind of mandatory when you're part of Hollywood, no matter what age you are. Like I said, it's all one big fucking show, and that's why I don't visit as much as I probably should."

"I guess I can appreciate that," she said.

I unlocked the doors. "You just wait until tonight. You'll never be back."

She stared at me curiously for a few seconds and then smiled.

"We'd better go inside," I said.

She laughed. "I guess we should."

As we slid out of the car, a dark sedan pulled up behind us.

"Good afternoon," smiled a thin, middle-aged man with light blonde hair, a thick moustache, and dark glasses. "I'm Pastor Richie."

I shook his hand. "I'm Reed Eddington and this is Sinclair –"

"Jeffries," she added, smiling at the pastor.

He shook her hand, too. "It's nice to meet you both. I'm here to speak with Mimi or Jack Eddington."

"Oh," I said. "Is everything okay?"

He smiled. "I believe so. I'm helping them renew their vows this evening."

My eyebrows shot up. "Really?"

"Yes. I spoke to Mimi this morning about it."

"Well, follow us," I said, walking towards the house. "I'm sure she's inside somewhere, directing the pre-party chaos."

***

Sinclair

I excused myself as soon as we entered the house, to go search for Jesse. Unfortunately, he wasn't in his bedroom or anywhere else in the house. Then, when I tried texting him, he didn't respond and I really became nervous.

"Have you seen Jesse?" I asked George, who was carrying a box of booze into the house.

"I'm sorry, I've been unloading some supplies for tonight. Have you checked the pool?"

"No. I'll go and see if he's out there," I said. "Thanks, George."

I found my way to the courtyard, where the large Olympic-sized swimming pool sat. Unfortunately, it was empty. As I was about to go back inside, I noticed a small building on the other side of the pool. It looked like a sauna or cabana and I wondered if he'd decided to unwind in it. I walked around the pool, and as I placed my hand on the door handle, I could hear moaning. Worried that Jesse was inside crying, I pushed the door open to console him, only to freeze dead in my tracks.

"Yes..." moaned Sela, who was on her hands and knees, the top of her swimsuit pushed away from her breasts, the bottoms lying on the ground next to her. Kneeling behind her was Jack, his white ass pumping furiously as he held onto her tan hips.

Stunned and horrified, I quietly shut the door and hurried back to the house.

Chapter Fourteen

Sinclair

I went straight to my bedroom and sat down on the bed, wondering what the hell I should do. Obviously, it wasn't any of my business. I was just a guest in Jack's home.

What about Reed and Mimi? Shouldn't they know?

Reed wasn't exactly innocent, however. Not after the way we'd attacked each other in my bedroom.

I still felt sick to my stomach as I thought about Sela and Jack together. He was obviously a sick bastard – to not only be cheating on his wife, but to be doing it right in his house *and* with his son's fiancée.

Just like Jesse mentioned, he *was* an asshole.

And Sela...

Well, it just substantiated my already negative feelings about her.

Sighing, I got out of bed and tried calling Jesse again, wondering where in the hell he was.

***

Reed

After leading Pastor Richie to my mother, who was in the kitchen making plans with the caterer, I went upstairs to check on Sela. Unfortunately, she wasn't around. I called her cell phone.

"Hello," she answered, sounding slightly winded.

"I'm back. You still by the pool?"

"Yes, I'll be right up."

"Okay, I'm in your room." I hung up, collapsed onto her bed, and turned on the television. A few minutes later, she breezed into the bedroom, engulfing me with the smell of coconuts and mango.

"Hi," she said, leaning over to kiss my lips.

"Hi. How'd it go?" I asked.

Her eyes widened. "How did *what* go?"

I yawned. "Relaxing, swimming, working on your tan... how did it go?"

She walked over to her suitcase and started rifling through it. "Okay. I'm full of chlorine and tanning oil. I'm going to take a shower."

I started flipping through the channels. "Good idea."

"Reed, I'm starving," she said, grabbing her shampoo. "Let's go someplace and eat."

I glanced at her. "I'm sorry, I just went to lunch. I'm sure Gretchen can fix you something. We'll go check with her when you're finished with the shower."

She put her hands on her hips and gave me a venomous look.

Oh shit.

"You went to lunch *without* me? I thought you were just doing a couple of errands," she snapped.

I shrugged. "I met up with Jesse and Sinclair. It wasn't something I'd planned to do *without* you, it just happened. Besides," I smiled. "What's one less salad in your life?"

"What in the hell is that supposed to mean?"

I turned off the television and stood up. "You hardly eat anything, Sela. Even if you would have joined us, you probably would have nibbled on vegetables and crackers."

She raised her chin in the air. "At least I wouldn't have been stuck here."

I stared at her incredulously. "I asked you if you wanted to join me today, but you declined."

Her lips thinned. "Well, you should have asked *harder.*"

Jesus Christ.

Her phone started vibrating and she grabbed it. After reading a text message, she looked at me. "Fine, if you're not going to take me anywhere, then could you find me something to eat while I'm in the shower?"

I nodded. "Sure, how about a sandwich?"

"I'd *prefer* a salad, tossed in vinaigrette dressing."

Sighing, I walked towards the door. "I'll see what I can find."

119

***

Sinclair

I finally got ahold of Jesse, who had driven all the way back to Alex's. Apparently, Alex had given him an ultimatum – either tell his parents about the two of them, or move on.

"He wants to marry me, Sin," he said. "But, the truth is, I'm not really ready for marriage. I mean, I care about him, a lot. But..."

"What are you going to do?" I asked.

"I don't know, yet. He's actually giving me a week to decide."

"What about your job? Are you going to have to leave the company?"

"He said I could stay, but our relationship would have to be totally platonic."

"But that would be..."

"Awkward," he said.

"Obviously. Well, at least he's not being a total asshole about it."

Jesse sighed. "He's a good guy but he just doesn't understand, I'm only twenty-four and he's thirty-six. I'm not ready for that kind of commitment yet."

"Then you'd better not do it," I said. "If you do it just to make him happy, it will never work. You'll both be miserable in the long run and you'll end up hating each other."

He sighed. "My thoughts exactly. I just needed to hear it from someone else."

"You're um... driving back to your parents', right?"

"I'll be back before the party. I want to try and talk to him a little more. Try to somehow reason with him."

"Okay. Don't forget, you still have my dress and shoes for tonight's party in your trunk, though."

He swore under his breath. "Okay, I'll be home by six at the latest."

"Thanks," I said. "Hey, there's something else," I said.

He paused. "What?"

I thought about everything he had on his plate at the moment, and decided to wait. "I'll tell you later, it's not important."

He snorted. "My dad didn't hit on you, did he?"

"I... ah... no," I said.

"Good. If he does, you have my permission to slug him."

"Okay," I said.

"And stay away from Mimi until the party starts. She's going to be going nuts, getting everything ready."

"Maybe I should try and help her out?"

"God forbid, don't even offer. This is her show and she won't even appreciate your offer. Just relax, go for a walk, or stay in the room until I get back."

I sighed. "Okay."

"Sin, I'm sorry about taking off like this," he said.

"No, it's okay," I said. "I get it. Really I do."

"Thanks, sweetie, I'll see you in a few."

After hanging up, I couldn't help but agonize over the horrible scene in the sauna. When it was all said and done, I decided to talk to Reed, since it was his right to know about Sela. If it was me, I would certainly want to know.

I left the bedroom and walked down the hallway towards his bedroom. As I raised my hand to knock, I heard someone clear their throat and turned my head.

"Miss me already?" asked Reed, coming towards me, holding a tray of food.

I blushed. "Um, no I just needed to talk to you."

"Okay. I have to take this salad back to Sela's room first."

Before I could answer, Sela walked out of *her* bedroom. "Oh, there you are..."

He handed her the tray of food. "I'll be right back, Sinclair needs to talk."

Sela turned and glared at me. "*You* need to talk? Where's Jesse?"

"He had to check in at work," I said. "But he should be back soon."

"Well, I'm sure you two can talk in front of me," she said, her lips thinned. "Reed and I have no secrets."

Right.

He stared at me and must have noticed something in my expression. He turned back to

Sela. "I'm sure it's about Jesse. Why don't you finish your lunch and I'll be back as soon as I can?"

She frowned. "Make it quick. We've had hardly any time to ourselves."

"It won't take long," I said.

She glared at me one last time, then turned and slammed the bedroom door.

Reed winced. "Sorry about that. She's a little sensitive."

"That's a nice way to put it."

He walked over to me and smiled. "So, your bedroom or mine?"

"How about by the pool?" I said.

"The pool?"

I nodded.

Yes, near the scene of the crime.

***

Reed

I followed Sinclair out to the pool, staring in awe at the way her ass moved in her shorts. It seemed to taunt me with every step.

"So," she said, sitting down at one of the poolside tables. "I don't even know how to tell you this..."

I sat down across from her. "Don't worry, I hear it all the time."

She looked at me, shocked. "What?"

"You can't stop thinking about me," I said, grinning broadly. "I know, it's tough."

She sat back in the chair and sighed. "Somehow I think you're going to get through this just fine."

I raised my eyebrows. "Get through what?"

"Reed!" hollered Jack, waving from patio. "Mimi needs you!"

"Can it wait?" I yelled.

He shook his head. "No, she needs you right now."

"Shit," I said, standing up. "I'll be right back. Don't move."

"Okay," she said.

I walked back towards the house. "What does she need?"

"Go and find out," he said, taking a sip of brandy or whatever the fuck he was drinking now. "She's in the dining room."

"Fine."

Jack rubbed the side of his moustache and motioned towards Sinclair. "Where's Jesse?"

"I'm not sure."

"Huh. Well, I'll keep Sinclair busy until you get back," he said, stepping off of the deck.

I glanced back towards Sinclair, who looked less than pleased to see Jack walking towards her.

***

Sinclair

124

Crap, what in the hell does he want? I thought, watching as Jack approached.

"Mind if I join you?" he asked.

"Go ahead," I said, wishing he'd just go away.

Instead, he sat down right next to me.

He raised his glass. "Would you care for a drink?"

"No thanks," I said, looking towards the house.

He drank the rest of his and set it down on the table. "So..."

I looked back at him and tried to hide my revulsion. He repelled me; made my skin crawl.

Jack glanced back towards the house and then his eyes shifted back to me. He licked his lips. "So, *Sinn*... did you enjoy the show in the sauna?"

My eyes widened in shock.

"You could have joined us, you know," he said with a wolfish grin.

I stood up, totally appalled. "That's sick."

"Sit down," he demanded sharply.

Stunned by the acid in his tone, I obeyed, like a small child.

"Now," he said, his eyes pinning me to the chair. "You're going to keep your mouth *shut*. If you say one word to anyone, you'll regret it. I have connections everywhere and trust me – you *don't* want to fuck with me. You got that, sweetheart?"

I opened my mouth, but couldn't speak.

"You got that?" he growled. "I'm not fucking around here. Answer me!"

I nodded vehemently.

He relaxed, his entire demeanor changed, and I wondered if he was psychotic.

"Good," he said, grinning like the Cheshire cat. "Because I can also make things very good for you, too. You're a beautiful girl, and as you witnessed earlier, I enjoy beautiful girls."

Bile rose in the back of my throat as his eyes raked over my body.

"You're not from around here, so I'm sure you have no idea how powerful I am. But," he smiled smugly. "I'm a fucking *king* in these parts, so, having me as a friend is to your benefit. You need a favor – anything, you come to Jack. A small loan, some financial advice, a little company..."

"Never," I whispered, hoarsely.

His face darkened. "Well, I can see that you need some time to understand the gravity of this situation. While you do that," he said, standing up, "I'm going to go and mix myself another drink. Would you like one?"

I shook my head.

"Fine," he said, swaying slightly. "Your loss."

As he walked back towards the house, I looked down at my hands and noticed they were trembling. I stood up and went inside to my room, not wanting to be around when the sociopath returned.

Chapter Fifteen

Reed

When I located Mimi, she was still with Pastor Richie.

"Hello, mother. Jack said you needed me for something?"

She looked confused. "No, I don't think so."

"Huh, well, okay. Sorry for the interruption," I said, turning to leave.

"Wait, Reed," she said, patting the cushion next to her on the sofa. "Come and introduce yourself to Pastor Richie."

"We met outside," said Pastor Richie, smiling.

I nodded. "Yes, we did. So, I hear you're going to be renewing your vows tonight, mother."

"Yes. At exactly ten o'clock tonight, under the moonlight," she sighed dreamily. "The same exact time we were married in Vegas."

"Does Jack know he's getting married again?" I asked. As far as I was concerned, he was unaware that he was married now.

"I mentioned it to him, yes," she said.

"Well, I'm very happy for the both of you," I said. "I'm sorry I can't stay, I've got some things to do. Please excuse me."

"Of course," said Mimi.

"It was nice meeting you, Pastor," I said. "I'm sure we'll have a chance to talk later."

"Indeed," said the Pastor.

I left them and went back outside to find Sinclair, who, unfortunately, was no longer sitting by the pool. As I turned to go back into the house and find her, Jack stepped back outside, his glass refilled.

"Do you know where Sinclair is?" I asked.

He shrugged. "Not sure. Maybe she's already preparing for tonight's party?"

I stared at him, wondering if he'd somehow scared her off. "So, getting your vows renewed this evening, huh, Jack?"

He smiled. "Yes, I guess we are."

"Hopefully you'll honor them a little better, this time around."

His face darkened. "What in the hell is that supposed to mean?"

I smiled, coldly. "I think you know very well what it means."

"You don't know shit," he said. "You just wait until *you're* married and then we'll talk."

"I may not be married yet, but I know that when you are, you keep your dick in your pants around other women."

He stared at me for a minute and then sighed. "Do you honestly think that I'm the only one who has strayed?"

"What is that supposed to mean?"

"Mimi," he answered. "She's had her share of flings over the years."

"Right."

"Listen, you can believe what you want, but let me tell you something, your mother isn't a saint, either."

"As far as I'm concerned, anyone who has put up with your shit all of these years, *is* a saint."

He took a sip of his drink but didn't respond.

Sighing, I left him on the deck and went back into the house to search for Sinclair.

***

Sinclair

I was pacing in my room, wondering if I should stay or call a cab, when there was a soft tap on my door. I opened it.

Reed.

"Can I come in?"

"Sure," I said, stepping aside.

"You okay?" he asked, turning to face me.

"I'm fine," I said, wondering what I was going to say to him now that Jack had basically threatened my future. I wasn't sure if he really had that much power, but I decided quickly that it wasn't worth finding out.

He sat down at the edge of my bed and grinned up at me. "So, now that you have me alone, what can I do for you?"

"I, um..."

His icy blue eyes slid down my body, giving me goose bumps. "What did you want to tell me?" he asked, softly.

I sighed. "It was nothing. I was concerned about Jesse, but now he's on his way back. Everything's fine."

"Oh, okay, that's good news."

"It is."

He stood up and moved towards me. "Question for you…"

"What?" I asked, looking up into his eyes.

He raised his fingers to my lips and gently lifted away a strand of my hair. "Christ," he whispered, staring at my mouth.

"What?" I asked, hardly able to breathe.

He was so close I could feel the warmth of his breath on my cheek. His eyes darkened and for a second, I thought he was going to kiss me. Instead, he sighed and took a step backwards. "Did Jack make any moves on you?"

I cleared my throat. "No. Why do you ask?"

"Because he does shit like that. In fact, he's hit on almost every woman I've brought home."

"That's despicable," I said. As far as I was concerned, Jack was a parasite.

He nodded. "Yes. So, if he does *anything* to make you uncomfortable, make sure that you tell me."

"Okay."

"I'm serious, especially tonight. Once he's had a few, you'll want to avoid him."

"I will," I said.

"I suppose I should get back to Sela. I'm glad to hear that Jesse is doing better now. That's a relief."

"Yeah, it is. He should be back in a couple of hours."

"Okay," said Reed, walking towards the door. "If you need anything before Jesse gets home, come and find me."

"Thanks, Reed."

He stared at me for a few seconds longer, then turned and walked out of the bedroom.

Chapter Sixteen

Sinclair

"I'm sorry I took off the way I did, Sin," said Jesse, arriving in my room with a flourish a couple of hours later. He held up the shopping bags. "Here are your new clothes, by the way."

"Thanks. So how did everything go?" I asked.

Jesse sighed. "Well, he's still pressuring me, but I did a lot of thinking on my way back and have decided to just end it with him."

I raised my eyebrows. "Really? What about your job?"

"I'll find another one. At least I still have the money coming in every month from my parents."

"Yeah, lucky you."

"So," he sat down on the bed. "Any problems when I was gone?"

Knowing that he'd cause a scene if I told him about Sela, I decided not to confide in anyone about what I'd witnessed. "No problems."

"Cool. Look, I'm going to take a shower and change."

"When does the party start?" I asked.

"Eight. Most of the guests won't arrive until later.

"Okay."

"Thanks again for helping me out, Sin," he said, kissing the top of my head. "I owe you, big."

I smiled. "Damn right you do."

"Seriously, though… tonight should be quite the show. It'll be fun."

"Okay."

As far as I was concerned, however, this night wouldn't go by fast enough. I'd had quite enough of Huntington Beach.

***

Less than two hours later, Jesse walked back into my bedroom dressed in a long-sleeved white-collared Dior shirt and black dress pants.

"Ready to tie one on before the party?" he asked, holding out two bottles of white wine. "I grabbed these two from the cellar; the old man will never even notice they're missing."

"I'll have a glass," I said, smoothing down my dress. "And go from there."

He put the bottles down on the dresser and turned to me. "Looking glamorous, Sin."

I smiled. "Thank you. You look pretty dashing yourself."

He kissed my cheek. "Thanks."

As he poured each of us a glass, I made one final inspection in the mirror. My hair was swept into a loose up-do, I'd applied extra makeup to my eyes, and the red dress fit like a glove. Personally, I didn't think I'd looked this nice at my senior prom.

"Toast – to the sexiest couple at the party," he said, raising his glass. "May we piss off the bitches and raise some cocks a few inches."

I smiled as we clinked our glasses together, still secretly hoping that one in particular would be raised, even if it wasn't mine to enjoy.

***

Reed

"Jesus, don't start this now, woman," I said to Sela, who was having a conniption because the heel of her right Jimmy Choo was somehow cracked. "You have four other pairs of shoes to choose from."

"But *these* go with my dress," she pouted. "None of the other pairs will work."

"Look at this," I said, pulling a pair of black high-heels from the bottom of her suitcase. "Why won't these work?"

"You just don't understand," she said, snatching them from me. "My dress is the color of champagne and the black shoes would never look right."

"So, what are you saying?" I asked.

Her lips curled under in disgust. "I'm just going to have to wear the blue and black dress now, I guess, which was supposed to be my *backup*."

"I'm sure you'll look gorgeous in either dress."

"Shit, shit, shit! This night is already ruined," she hollered, throwing the broken-heeled shoe across the room.

"Calm down, Sela. It will be fine," I said. "You'll still look beautiful and nobody will care if your dress is gold, black, or even pea-green."

"You just don't understand," she said. "I've worn the blue dress before. I've *never* worn the champagne one."

I sighed. "Look, I'm going back to change into my suit. The one I *have* worn in the past and will definitely wear in the future, and frankly, my dear, I don't give a fuck if anyone notices."

She scowled at me, grabbed her blue dress, and slammed the bathroom door for the umpteenth time.

I shook my head. If this was how she acted in the beginning of a relationship, I couldn't imagine what it would be like when the honeymoon was over. Thankfully, I wouldn't be the unfortunate guy to find out.

Chapter Seventeen

Michael

The party was well on its way by the time I arrived. I handed over my keys to the valet, who must not have thought I could see his smirk as he got into the driver's seat. But, I didn't care because I knew that I would be the one enjoying myself inside while he spent the rest of the evening, parking cars – ones he would never own. Not only that, but *I* would be leaving tonight with the most beautiful girl at the party. My cock was already twitching as I fantasized about all of the glorious things we would do together once she was in my bed.

No more waiting.

Half-hard, I stepped into the house and through the crowd. As I scanned the bodies of people, I was quite amazed at the turnout. Although the Eddingtons are older, most of the guests appeared to be in their twenties and thirties. Many even celebrities.

"Oh, excuse me," I said to a tall, blonde woman with short spiky hair as my hand brushed against her cute little ass.

When she turned to look at me, she obviously believed it was an accident and flashed me one of her famous smiles. "No problem," she said in a familiar, husky voice.

I thought back to her last movie and the scene where she was naked, in bed. Although she was quite lovely herself, she still didn't hold a candle to my beautiful, sexy Sinclair.

Thinking of Sinclair, I quickly looked through the crowd for my lovely goddess, but she was nowhere to be found. As I finagled my way through the many guests, I noticed that most were already drinking booze or openly indulging in other forms of mood-enhancing paraphernalia. One young musician stared at me in horror as he tried to wipe away a dusting of white powder from his nose. I pretended not to notice and continued moving.

"Oh, there you are," smiled Mimi, stepping away from a group of older ladies in the large formal dining room. "I was getting worried about you."

"I'm terribly sorry," I said. "Traffic was bad. There was some kind of accident and it took me much longer than anticipated."

Mimi nodded. "Well, I'm glad you made it, back. Let me introduce you to all of my friends." She then pulled me over to her group of cronies and smiled. "Ladies, let me introduce you to Pastor Richie."

***

Sinclair

Jesse and I ended up playing cards in my bedroom and drinking a little more wine than what *I'd* originally planned. By the time it was eight-thirty, both of us were feeling slightly tipsy.

He held out his arm for me to take. "Ready, fairest princess?" he asked with a lopsided grin.

"Yes, fairest queen," I said, trying to steady myself on the high heels.

He threw his head back and laughed. "Oh, we are going to be out of control tonight. I can just tell this is going to be fun."

I put my hand on his arm and gave him a serious look. "Just remember to stick with me," I said. "Don't go sniffing after any hot guys and leaving me all on my own."

"I'll try but if I reach a breaking point, I'll let you know."

"You'd better behave or your parents might catch on. You can't afford to lose that extra money, especially now."

He sighed. "Very true. Well, let's go crash this party and liven things up."

***

Reed

"So, you're really getting married?" pouted Sherry, a pretty redhead I'd dated a few times in my early twenties.

"Ah, yeah," I said, trying to get out of the corner she'd backed me into. Thank goodness Sela was too busy schmoozing with some of the producers Jack had invited, in another area of the house. She was obviously still trying to get into the movies.

"Too bad," she smiled, trailing a long red nail along my forearm. "I'm so damn horny tonight and my husband is out of town."

"Well, I'm sure there are plenty of available men here would –"

It was then that I noticed *her* moving down the staircase.

Sinclair.

Jesus.

She was a vision of beauty in a red dress that hugged every curve of her voluptuous body. With every step she took, a flash of thigh peeked out from a slit in the gown, making it harder for me to breathe as I pictured my hand on that pale skin. When her sparkling green eyes finally met mine, she smiled and everyone else in the room ceased to exist.

"Reed?" said Sherry.

I cleared my throat. "Excuse me," I answered, stepping away.

"Hey, Reed," said Jesse as I met him at the bottom of the stairs. "Nice turnout, huh?"

"Definitely," I said, still staring into Sinclair's eyes. "Magnificent, better than I could have ever imagined."

Sinclair's cheeks turned pink and she lowered her eyelashes.

"So, where's that shrew of yours?" asked Jesse.

It was a struggle not to openly gape at Sinclair's cleavage. I turned to my brother instead. "Sela? She's around."

"Wonderful," he replied dryly. "I'm thirsty. Sinclair, would you like another glass of wine?"

"No, I'm okay right now," she said.

"Party pooper," he said, giving her a pouty look. "You sure?"

"I'd better not," she said. "You know how I get when I've had a little too much to drink."

I raised an eyebrow. "How do you get, Sinclair?"

She smiled. "Wouldn't you like to know?"

"I'll tell you how she gets – rowdy, loud, and uninhibited," said Jesse, a small smile playing on his lips.

"In that case," I said. "Find us a couple of bottles."

She shook her head and laughed.

"Listen, I'll be right back. I'll bring you back a wine cooler, in case you change your mind," said Jesse, leaving Sinclair alone with me.

"Nice," she said. "I told him not to abandon me and he does it right away."

"Don't worry, Sin," I said, resisting the urge to pick her up and carry her away to my bedroom. "You're in good hands with me."

She opened her mouth to say something, but then changed her mind.

"What?" I asked, taking a sip of my beer.

"Nothing," she said, shaking her head, although the sparkle in her eyes told me something otherwise.

My eyes slid back down to her leg, which was peeking through the slit once again. I thought about both of those legs wrapped around my waist and took another swig of beer.

"Nice dress by the way," I said, my voice sounding slightly hoarse.

"Thanks."

"Jesse better keep a close eye on you in that or someone's bound to throw you over their shoulder and head for the nearest cave."

She laughed. "Oh, you think so?"

I smiled wickedly. "Are you kidding? A woman like you in a dress like that?"

She pushed me playfully. "You're terrible."

"Now that's one thing I've never been called."

Her eyes raked quickly over my body and then she blushed. "So," she asked, changing the subject. "Where are your parents?"

I shrugged. "They're around. Jack's probably in a dark corner, groping some young starlet and mom, well, she's probably in the kitchen gossiping with friends."

She rubbed the corner of her eye and blinked. "Darn it."

"What?"

"I, um... I have to use the ladies room. I knew this was going to happen when I started drinking."

I stood up straighter. "Do you want me to follow you?"

She laughed. "No, I think I know where the nearest one is by now."

I nodded. "Okay. I'll be waiting right here with Jesse when you return."

"Thanks."

I watched as she walked away, her nicely rounded hips swaying as she left. I took another pull of my beer.

Chapter Eighteen

Sinclair

I walked away from Reed, relieved that he didn't follow me. He looked so handsome in his dark wool suit and smelled absolutely... amazing. After two glasses of wine and catching his fiancée cheating, I knew there wouldn't be any resistance left in me. If he as so much made any more sexual innuendos towards me, I'd more than likely pull him into the nearest closet and make him forget about the rest of the world. But for now, I just wanted to check my makeup, not really having to pee. I had this feeling that my eyeliner had run and that I really needed to fix it.

I moved through the crowd towards the bathroom, noticing that some of the faces were familiar – a couple of famous actors, a very infamous musician, and even a couple of models that were no longer in their prime but still beautiful. As I was about to enter the bathroom, someone grabbed my arm and pulled me back.

"Hey, gorgeous," said a tall, blond musician type-of-guy covered in tats and piercings.

"Oh, hi," I said, suddenly recognizing the hunky singer who I'd seen in concert as a teenager. "Look, I..."

"Where in the hell has Jack been hiding you?" he asked with a lazy grin, his eyes trailing over my dress. "Are you an actress?"

My cheeks turned pink. "No," I beamed up at him, unable to help myself. He was just as sexy off-stage, as on.

He leaned closer. "Not an actress, that's cool. Do you um... party?" he asked.

I bobbed my head up and down. "Yes, I mean I've had a couple of drinks, already. That's why I'm headed towards the bathroom, actually."

He threw his head back and laughed. "You're too fucking cute."

"Well, thanks. So are you," I gushed. "Listen, I..."

He grabbed my hand and started pulling me away from my original destination. "This way, you sexy little thing."

Although I still wanted to check my makeup, I couldn't help but be flattered that this famous singer wanted to have a drink with me. I knew the girls at *Tangled* were going to be so freakin' amazed when I told them about it. As I pictured their shocked faces, we stopped abruptly.

"Going somewhere?" asked Reed, blocking our path.

"Oh, hey – Reed, isn't it?" said the singer. "Yeah, man, we're going to have ourselves a little one-on-one time. Can we use one of your bedrooms?"

Reed's eyebrows shot up.

"Bedroom?" I pulled my hand away and glared up at him. "You said *party.* I thought that meant an innocent little drink."

The singer's face darkened. "Looks like you have a little attitude. Glad I found out now before you busted my balls later."

When he walked away, I turned to Reed, who looked rather pissed.

"What?" I asked.

"You have no idea what kind of party he was talking about, do you?"

"Apparently not."

Reed looked around and then grabbed my elbow. "I see now that I can't let you out of my sight. Let's go."

"I still have to use the bathroom," I mumbled as we started moving through the crowded room.

"Bathroom?" He swore under his breath and then changed our course towards the kitchen. "You can use the one near the pantry. It should be free."

"Okay."

We entered the kitchen, where it was *crazy* busy. Several people were preparing trays of hors d'oeuvres or pouring glasses of champagne, while the wait-staff bustled in and out, grabbing them on the fly.

"Excuse us," said Reed as he maneuvered me out through the back entrance and then down a long corridor which must have led to the pantry. Thankfully the hallway was dark and quiet compared to the rest of the house.

Reed suddenly stopped and turned to face me, his eyes holding me with an intensity that sent shivers down my spine.

"Well, um thanks," I murmured, trying to figure out why he still looked angry.

He stepped closer to me, his face strained. "What in the fuck are you doing to me?" he whispered, hoarsely.

Before I could ask what he meant, he slid one of his hands into the back of my hair and reeled me in.

***

Reed

The thought of her and the musician together unglued me. As far as I was concerned, if anyone was going to have some one-on-one time with Sinclair, it would be me.

I pulled her into my arms and claimed her lips with a vengeance. When she didn't protest and opened her mouth to mine, I groaned and pushed her back against the wall, wanting to devour her. Remembering how excited I'd gotten her earlier was making my cock throb with anticipation. I needed to be inside of her, right now. *Fuck the rest of the world.*

***

Sinclair

His tongue was demanding as it moved into my mouth and I responded like a ravenous animal, devouring and encouraging him to give me more.

I slid my hands into the back of his hair, my fingers wrapping around the strands, pulling and tugging, trying to draw our hungry mouths closer.

I just couldn't get enough of him.

One of his hands moved to my left breast, sliding into the deep neckline, claiming it with a rumbling groan in the back of his throat as he cupped it tightly.

I let out a soft moan as he pinched and rolled my nipple between his fingertips. It was as if an electric current was sending sexually-charged tingles to the junction between my legs, creating an ache so intense that I knew I was now totally at his mercy.

And loving every minute of it.

I was on fire as his lips moved to my neck while his other hand moved up the slit of the dress, to my leg. My breath caught in my throat as his hand began to stroke my inner thigh, slowly moving towards the place that I needed him the most. When his fingers brushed the side of my panties, I dug my nails into the back of his neck and closed my eyes, aching for his touch.

"Reed," I whimpered in agony as he ran his finger very slowly over the outside of my panties.

It had been so long since I'd had anyone touch me in that spot that my panties were already drenched.

Noticing this, he let out a strangled groan and pushed them over to the side, exposing my most intimate spot.

"Oh..." I shuddered, as he cupped my mound and slid one of his fingers inside of me. I closed my eyes and spread my legs wider as his hand began to move, creating a familiar pressure inside of my pelvis that needed to be released.

"Sinclair," he whispered into my neck, as he made circular motions with the pad of his thumb on my sweet spot. "I need you..."

I closed my eyes. "Yes," I whimpered as his fingers moved faster, making my legs shake.

"Hold on," he said, removing his hand. Before I knew what was happening, his jacket was off, he was on his knees, and his tongue was making a hot, wet trail up my inner thigh.

Ohmygod...

My legs felt like jelly and my stomach muscles clenched up as his tongue continued its torment, moving closer and closer to its destination.

"Reed," I whispered, holding on to the back of the wall as he kissed and flicked his tongue along my inner thigh. I wanted to grab him by the hair and pull him into my heat – he was moving much too slow and I was aching for his tongue. "Please," I begged again.

Our eyes met and he grinned wickedly. He knew *exactly* what he was doing to me.

Reed positioned my legs even farther apart and then his tongue moved to the edge of my panties, still taunting me. He pulled them over to the side with his finger again and I knew it would only take one or two slow, steady strokes in the center and I'd be pulling his hair and screaming out his name. As I waited for the firm, wet pressure from that glorious tongue of his, the echo of voices drew near, startling us both.

"Shit," he growled, shooting up.

Trying to compose myself, I released a ragged breath and pulled my dress down.

"Bathroom," he ordered, pushing me towards it. "Hurry."

I shut the door behind me just as I heard Mimi addressing her oldest son.

Chapter Nineteen

Reed

"What are you doing back here?" asked my mother. "We've been looking all over for you."

I cleared my throat. "What's going on?" I asked, moving towards her, holding my jacket in front of me.

"Sela is getting out of control," she said. "And Pastor Richie is about to start the ceremony. Come on."

I frowned. "Sela is out of control?"

She sighed. "Yes. I'm not sure what's going on with that girl but she's acting rather strange."

I nodded. "Okay, I'll be right there."

"She's in the great-room. Please do something about her." Then she turned and walked back towards the kitchen.

Sinclair pushed the door open, quietly. "Is everything okay?" she asked.

I smiled. "Oh, just the same old shit," I said. "Sela, acting out."

She looked away, avoiding my eyes. "We'd better get back."

I went to her. "I want you to know something," I said, raising her chin up to meet my gaze. "I'm not marrying Sela. There's no way."

She bit her lower lip. "I'm sorry."

My eyes widened. "You have nothing to be sorry about. Meeting you has opened my eyes and turned me back in the right direction. Jesus, I'm grateful."

"But –"

I put a finger to her lips to quiet her. "I'm not ready for marriage, especially with Sela. To be truthful, I'm not even sure why either of us wanted it to begin with. She's not in love with me and I'm definitely not in love with her."

She gave me a stunned look. "You don't love each other?"

I chuckled and pulled her against my chest. "Not at all. Jesus, I've felt more in the last few hours with you then I've felt the past few months with Sela."

She released a long sigh. "So, it's not my fault."

"Well, it's your fault I'm harder than a rock, but I won't hold it against you."

"I'll gladly take responsibility for that," she whispered.

I kissed her lips and sighed. "I'd love to continue this, but if we don't get back, Sela AND my mother are going to raise the roof."

"We should find Jesse, too," she said.

I smiled. "Of course. We don't want your boyfriend getting jealous."

"Come on, you've already figured that out."

I raised my eyebrows. "Figured what out?"

She licked her lips. "That –"

"That he's been gay his entire life and you two are trying to pull the wool over my parents' eyes. Why, is the real question."

"He doesn't want your parents to know."

151

"That's what I figured. Why in the hell not?"

"He's afraid they'll cut out his trust fund money."

"That won't happen," I said. "They have no control over that money. It was left for us by our grandparents."

"Doesn't he understand that?" she asked.

"I thought he did. I guess I was wrong."

"Well, you'd better let him know."

"No," I said, smiling. "It's more entertaining watching you two."

"That's cruel."

"Not giving me another kiss before we go back, is what's cruel," I said, pulling her into my arms.

Fortunately, Sinclair isn't cruel

Chapter Twenty

Sinclair

Reed and I returned to the party, which had moved outside for Mimi and Jack's ceremony.

"Where have you been?" asked Jesse, standing next to the sauna, drinking a wine-cooler. He didn't appear upset in the least that I'd been gone for so long. When I noticed the cute group of young men he was standing with, I understood why.

"Sorry. Had to use the bathroom," I said.

"Princess Puddles, should have known," he teased. "I drank your wine-cooler by the way. It was getting warm. Sorry, sweetie."

"No problem," I answered. I was finished drinking for the rest of the night.

"I suppose I'd better go find Sela," muttered Reed, his eyes scouring the crowd of people. Most were either standing around the pool or sitting at the tables, drinking and socializing. Others were playing dice or cards.

"Check the house," said Jesse, a strange smile on his face. "She was in there with Barry Goldberg, talking about her up and coming 'acting career'."

Reed rolled his eyes. "Okay, thanks,"

"See you later," I said.

He turned to me and his lips curled into a secretive grin. "I'd like to continue that discussion we had earlier."

"I'd like that, too," I said, my cheeks turning warm.

"Good. I'm sure we can get a little more in depth this time."

I didn't trust myself to answer, so I just nodded and then watched as he retreated back to house, already missing him.

"Sin, I have someone I'd like you to meet," said Jesse, turning to a tall, handsome guy who looked familiar. "This is that actor I was telling you about."

Ah...the actor who'd taken his virginity.

"Oh, obviously I recognize you," I said, shaking his hand. "I loved your last movie, when you were that double-agent."

The actor smiled and his teeth were so white, they glowed. "Thank you. Are you an actress?"

I shook my head. "No."

"She's my date," said Jesse, putting an arm around my waist.

The actor stared at me, appraisingly. "Now that's interesting. Maybe the both of you would like to join me for a drink on my yacht later?"

The look in his eyes told me he wanted us to join him for more than just a drink.

"I don't think..." I stammered.

"She won't be able to," interrupted Jesse. "But I'm game."

"Excellent," he said, finishing his drink. "We'll talk more about it after this so-called wedding."

After he walked away, Jesse pulled me in closer to whisper into my ear. "Did see how hot he looked? Oh, my God, I want to jump his freakin' bones."

I giggled. "You'll probably get the chance, on his *yacht*."

He sighed. "Maybe. It kind of made me feel ookie that he wanted both of us, though. Obviously, it was for more than a measly drink."

"I know what you mean."

"Oh, fuck-it," chuckled Jesse. "I'll do him. I've been fantasizing about a reunion with that guy for years."

I cleared my throat. "Speaking of that, Jesse, we really need to talk." I wanted to tell him about the trust fund so he could relax about it.

His eyes widened. "Oh, my, my, my, sounds serious, Sin, but it will have to wait. I see two of mother's old crony friends coming our way." He turned towards them as they approached. "Betty and Charlotte! So glad you could make it."

Jesse stuck with me and we mingled with some of the other guests. As the crowd became more boisterous and rowdy, I started wondering what was taking so long for the ceremony. It was getting late and I hadn't seen Mimi or Jack around lately.

"I thought your parents were getting re-married soon," I said to Jesse.

He looked at his watch and frowned. "Hmm...it's getting late. Let's go find out what's happening with the two little lovebirds."

I followed him through the yard and back into the house.

"George, have you seen my parents?" asked Jesse, as the butler walked out of the kitchen.

He wiped his forehead with a handkerchief. "No, sorry, sir, I've been in the kitchen trying to figure out what's wrong with the water pipes, some of them are leaking."

"Oh. Well, I'll let mother know if we find her. Have you called a professional?" asked Jesse.

George sighed. "It's late. We're just going to have to live with it until the morning."

"Oh, that sucks. Maybe you should have a drink or something, George," said Jesse. "Relax for a few minutes."

"If only it were that easy," said George with a pained expression as he walked away.

"Should we check to see if Mimi is getting ready?" I said. I knew if it was me, I'd be probably be primping before the event.

"Good idea," he said.

We walked up the stairs to his parents' bedroom and knocked on the door, but it was quiet and nobody responded. Jesse pushed the door open and glanced inside. "Hello! Anyone alive in here?" When Mimi didn't answer, he turned to me. "They could be in Jack's office. It's also through here."

I followed him inside and stared in appreciation at Jack and Mimi's spacious bedroom. It appeared larger than my apartment, with its built-in fireplace, large walk-in closet, and reading nook overlooking the ocean. When we reached a doorway on the other side of the bedroom, he stopped, abruptly. "Do you hear that?" he whispered.

From the grunts and moans on the other side of the door, it sounded like someone was having sex.

"Let's get out of here," he whispered, pulling my arm. "Wow, I thought the honeymoon happened after the wedding," laughed Jesse.

"I guess not on the second time around," I said, surprised that his parents were even having sex.

"Dammit," he said, looking down at his shirt. "I must have spilled some wine on it, earlier. Why didn't you tell me?" he pouted.

I stared at the small light-red speckles. "Sorry, I didn't even notice it myself."

"I'm going to my room and change, quickly. Why don't you wait for me downstairs?"

I nodded.

"Better yet," he said. "The library. Wait for me in there and we'll mix ourselves a couple of cocktails. My dad keeps his expensive stash in there."

"Sure," I said.

He grinned. "Just stay away from the north side of the library. He keeps his smut on that side."

I shuddered. "Good to know."

"Seriously, he gets into some really raunchy stuff," he said, walking back upstairs.

That doesn't surprise me, I thought, as I walked downstairs to the library. I opened the door and stepped inside.

"Didn't your mother ever teach you to knock before entering?" snapped Sela, standing next to a sofa, slipping on a pair of black heels.

"Oh, I'm sorry," I said, taking a step back. "I didn't realize that anyone was in here."

"It's okay," she said, straightening up. Her hair was slightly disheveled and her lips, swollen. "We're finished now, anyway."

I raised my eyebrows. "Finished?"

"Don't ask," she said, with a wicked grin. She walked over to a doorway on the other side of the room and knocked. "You'd better put your pants back on, *Reed*," she said, loudly. "We have company."

I felt like someone had kicked me in the stomach. He'd left me only to have sex with Sela.

"Sorry, I'll just leave," I said, moving towards the door.

"À bientôt!" called Sela.

What did you expect? I thought, to myself. *Sela is his fiancée. She's beautiful, successful, and rich. He was just using you for a quick piece of ass. Nothing more.*

Like father, like son.

Chapter Twenty-one

Sinclair

I was angry and disgusted with myself for being so naïve, so much that I didn't even notice Pastor Richie rounding the corner, and we collided.

"Oh, I'm sorry, Pastor," I apologized, as he grabbed my arm to help steady me.

He smiled. "It's quite all right. It's Sinclair, isn't it?"

"Yes," I said, as he released my arm.

"Well, I'm glad I ran into you. I could really use someone's help."

"Oh?"

He pushed his glasses up higher on his nose. "Yes, you see, I brought a special gift for the ceremony and it's very fragile. It's so delicate, in fact, that I don't even trust those young men parking the vehicles outside. They're so reckless with those cars and I should hate to have anything happen to the Eddington's gift."

"Oh, well I can certainly help you," I said. "No problem."

"Thank you, Sinclair," he beamed. "You're such an angel."

"I don't know about that," I chuckled, as we started walking towards the front door.

"Oh, you are. I can just tell with some people."

"Hey, Sinclair!" hollered Jesse, who was just coming down the stairs. "Where you going?"

I turned around. "I'm going outside to help Pastor Richie," I called back.

"Oh, well, okay. I'll fix you a drink and meet you out in the back."

"Thanks!" I hollered and turned back around to follow the pastor.

"I hope you don't mind walking up the block," said Pastor Richie. "I'm not going to make any of the valets drive my car back here just for a package."

"No," I said. "I can handle it."

We stepped outside and one of the valet drivers handed him his keys after we explained our mission.

"You sure?" asked the handsome young Italian man, who kept smiling at me. He was younger, maybe eighteen or nineteen. "I wouldn't want this lovely lady to break a heel."

"I'll be fine," I said, returning his smile.

"Yes, we'll be right back," said Pastor Richie. "It won't take long."

"Okay. Be careful, Miss," said the valet. "There's a dip at the end of the driveway."

"Thanks," I answered.

"My, he seemed to be taken with you," said Pastor Richie as we began walking.

"Oh," I smiled. "I doubt it."

"He is, believe me. I know that look."

I didn't answer. It didn't matter if the valet was interested in me or anyone else at the party. I didn't want to think about sex or men at the moment.

"Watch out," said Pastor Richie, pointing towards the uneven road. "There's that spot he was talking about. Here," he held out his arm. "Hold on to me."

"Thanks," I said, grabbing onto his elbow as I stepped over the divot. Once we'd cleared it, I began pulling my hand back when he stopped me.

"Just keep holding on," he said. "With those heels of yours, I'd hate to see you fall."

"Okay, thanks, Pastor," I said as we continued to walk. I had to admit, it felt good leaning on someone besides Jesse for a change. Besides, I needed more of a fatherly figure at the moment – someone strong and reliable. It was almost comforting.

"There it is," he said, pointing towards his car, which was parked towards the end of the block. "Looks like I didn't earn the VIP spot."

"I wouldn't have either if I'd have driven up in my two-thousand-and-four Malibu," I said. "They probably would have told me to keep driving."

He patted my hand. "I doubt that. You underestimate yourself. These people should be grateful that you attended their little party."

Grateful?

He was such a sweet man.

I smiled. "Well, I don't know about grateful, but..."

"Nonsense," he said, as we stopped behind the trunk of his car. "Those people, the Eddingtons, are snobby ingrates who don't understand the value of people or the true meaning of life."

I stared at him in surprise as he turned and opened up his trunk, an angry scowl on his face. I bit my lower lip. "I –,"

"It's okay," he interrupted, his face softening, again, "You don't have to pretend anymore, my love."

My what?

I cleared my throat and forced a smile. "Um, Pastor?"

He reached out a hand and touched my cheek as I stared at him in confusion. "You are so beautiful."

I took a step backwards. "What are you doing?"

He licked his lips. "Don't play coy, my dear. Now, call me Michael."

I noticed the look in his eyes, it looked anything but fatherly. "Michael?"

His eyes narrowed. "No, that's not right. Say it *softly... Michael.*"

The hair on the back of my neck stood straight up. Something was very wrong with this man. I quickly glanced towards his trunk, which didn't contain much more than a couple of pillows and a blanket. "What's going on here?"

His lips tightened. "Isn't it obvious? I've come for *you.* We can finally be together. Just like we were meant to be."

Horrified, I turned to leave, but he grabbed me around the waist and pulled me back.

"No!" I choked as his hand clamped over my mouth.

"Shh," he whispered into my ear, holding me against his body as I tried to struggle and break free. He was *so* much stronger than he looked. "I'm sorry," he said as his hand closed over my face, the smell of some strange chemical filling my nostrils. "Sleep, my love."

Chapter Twenty-two

Reed

"Where's Sinclair?" I asked Jesse.

"She's with Pastor Richie," he said. "But if she doesn't get back here soon, I'm drinking her rum and Coke. The ice is almost melted. Where've you been, by the way?"

I sighed. "The pipes are leaking in the kitchen. George and I have been in there for the last hour trying to fix the problem. It's a nightmare for the catering staff."

Jesse looked past me and scowled. "Oh, great, here comes the shrew."

I turned to find Sela heading right for us, followed by Jack, who looked inebriated.

Shit.

"Hi, lover," said Sela, putting her arms around my neck. "Where've you been all night?"

I grabbed her hands. "I've been around. The real question is, where've you been?"

"She was with me," slurred Jack, putting his arm around her shoulders. "Gettin' to know my new daughter-in-law."

I sighed. "Weren't you the one who was supposed to be getting married again?"

"Pfft...," he said, waving his arm. "Your mother is all bent out of shape about something, I don't even know what it is. Says to just forget about the whole vow thing."

"Really?" I asked, trying to control my temper. He obviously did something to hurt her again and from the way he was pawing Sela, it wasn't too difficult to figure out.

"Jack," said Sela, trying to unwind herself from his embrace. "You should really look for Mimi."

"Oh, she'll be fine," he said, swaying. "Hey, want to go for a swim?" he asked, tugging at his clothes.

"What the fuck are you doing?" I asked, stepping closer to him.

"Listen up!" hollered Jack, who was now removing his shoes. "The pool is now open for skinny-dipping! Don't be shy! Let's see some tits and ass!"

"Oh, my Gawd..." giggled Jesse. "Jack's completely wasted."

There were about sixty or so people, gathered around the pool watching Jack's little performance. Many of the younger guys were cheering him on while some of Mimi's friends looked completely horrified.

"Jack," I hissed, grabbing his arm. "Knock this shit off. You're making a fool out of yourself."

He shook my arm away. "Sela was right about you," he said, his eyes bloodshot. "You're a party pooper, a real fucking drag."

"Hey, I never said that!" cried Sela. She turned to me. "He is obviously drunk and doesn't know what he's saying!"

"Oh yeah," whispered Jack loudly. "It's between us."

"Enough," I said. "Jack, go back into the house before this episode gets more fucked up."

He brushed me off. "Oh, you're such a stick in the mud. I can see why Sela needs a little more excitement in her life."

"Okay, enough, dad," interrupted Jesse, looking mortified. "It's not funny anymore."

Jack ignored both of us as he staggered over to Sela and pulled her against him. He smiled drunkenly. "I may be higher than a kite, but I'll bet you've never been fucked that good by him, have you?" he whispered loudly into her ear.

I stormed over to him, ripped Sela out of his arms and got right into his face. "You really fucked up," I growled. "But the person you hurt more than anything this time around, is yourself."

Then I lifted him up into the air, walked over to the pool, and dropped him in.

Chapter Twenty-three

Sinclair

My skull felt like someone had hit it with a sledgehammer when I finally regained consciousness. As my mind began to clear, I realized that I was in someone's dingy basement, on a mattress which had been pushed to the corner of a laundry room. The place was dark, except for a small nightlight next to me, and had a weird smell, one that I couldn't quite figure out.

"Oh, my God," I shuddered, as the memories of the last few hours resurfaced.

I scrambled away from the mattress and hurried up the wooden steps.

"No," I moaned, jiggling the door, finding it locked.

Frantic, I went back downstairs to look for another way out and found a window above the dryer. I climbed on top and moved the curtain away, only to find the window boarded up.

Why? I wondered, trying to remain calm. *This guy was a man of the church, why in the name of God would he do something like this?*

As I stared outside through a small hole in the wood, I couldn't see anything but darkness and trees. I wondered if I was in some kind of cabin and what he meant to do with me. His talk of the two of us being together and the glazed look in his eyes had given me the chills. He was obviously insane.

The sound of someone whistling startled me. I looked around the room for something to defend myself with, but there was nothing but a jug of clothing detergent and a box of dryer sheets.

"Hello," smiled the Pastor as he walked down the steps carrying a tray of food. As he stepped closer, I was surprised to find that he'd undergone some major changes. He was now dressed in jeans and a black sweatshirt, his glasses were gone, and his moustache missing.

"What in the hell are you doing?" I blurted out. "Why did you kidnap me?"

He set the tray of food down on the nightstand. "I must admit, your language and anger are quite disturbing, my dear. Please calm down."

I stepped towards him. "Calm down?! Are you fucking nuts?"

His face turned red, and before I knew what was happening, his hand was around my neck and I was being slammed against the wall. "Shut up," he whispered, his eyes bulging out of his face.

My own were filled with tears as I struggled to break free, but he was much too strong. "Please," I gasped as his fingers dug deep into my neck.

"Please what?" he asked.

"Please," I begged in a hoarse whisper. "I beg you."

His eyes widened and he let me go, backing away. "I'm sorry," he said.

"Why?" I choked. "Why are you doing this?"

He took a step towards me. "I didn't mean... you shouldn't..."

I moved away from him. "Please, just leave me alone and let me go home."

He began wringing his hands. "No, no, no. This isn't going the way it was supposed to."

"Why are you doing this?" I tried again. "You're supposed to be a man of God, aren't you?"

"This has nothing to do with *God*," he said, his lips thinning.

"Obviously," I said, wondering if I should try to make a run for it.

"You still don't remember me?" he asked incredulously.

"Am I supposed to?"

He sighed. "From the salon. You cut my hair in the past, several times."

My eyes widened. I *had* cut his hair. The last time was about two months ago. But now, he looked so different.

Thinner.

"You've lost weight," I said.

He smiled and stood up straight. "Yes. I've lost about forty pounds. I did it for you."

I stared at him in horror. "For me? I just don't understand, why?"

He ignored the question. "Here," he said, pointing towards the tray of food. "Eat something. You're probably very hungry."

I licked my lips. Obviously he was crazy, but he was also obsessed with me. If I could somehow manipulate him...

"I have a headache, Pastor," I said, forcing a smile. "Do you have any aspirin?"

"Yes, of course," he said. "But call me Michael. I'm no longer a Pastor."

"Oh, okay. Michael, could you please get me something for this headache?"

"Yes. Would you like to come upstairs?"

"Sure," I said.

He reached into back of his pants and pulled out a set of handcuffs. "Okay, but I'll need to handcuff you first," he said, pulling a set out.

Crap.

"You don't need to use those," I said. "I'm not going to try and escape."

He smiled. "That's good, but I still can't take that chance. Hold out your hands."

"But..."

"The cuffs or you stay down here," he said. "Until we come to an understanding, at least."

"What kind of understanding?"

His eyes moved to my cleavage and I immediately understood.

"Oh, why didn't you just say so?" I asked. There was no way I'd have sex with this guy but I could at least hurt him.

He gave me a surprised look.

I took a step towards him and pushed out my chest, hoping he couldn't see the disgust in my eyes. "Michael."

He touched my cheek and I tried not to shrink back. "I knew you felt the same way," he beamed. "I just knew it."

"I did too, the moment I met you," I said. "In fact, I haven't been able to stop thinking about you."

"Would... would you touch me?" he asked, breathing a little harder.

"Where?" I whispered, hoping he had some kind of weird hair fetish and only really wanted my hands there.

He grabbed my hand and pressed it to his lips. "Touch me wherever you'd like," he whispered.

At that moment, I really wanted to just kick him in the balls and make a run for it, but I was still too frightened.

What if I missed or didn't kick him hard enough?

Instead, I placed a hand on his chest and began rubbing it. "Does this feel good?" I asked.

"Yes, oh yes," he said, stopping my hand with his. "But I need..." he lowered my hand to the bulge in his jeans, "you here."

I swallowed back the bile in my throat and forced myself to touch the disgusting thing hidden under his pants. If he had an orgasm, there was no doubt in my mind that I was going to throw up. I had to get out of this.

"Yes," he groaned, staring at me, his eyes half-hooded. "Now, take it out."

Oh God, no...

"Please," he said, unbuttoning his jeans. "Just touch... a little. It's all I ask."

I stared in revulsion as he pulled out his penis and began stroking it himself.

171

"I... I," I stammered, glancing up towards the stairs, wondering if I could make it.

He grabbed my hand and put it on his naked penis.

Horrified beyond belief, I reached down below his penis and grabbed his balls, squeezing them with everything I had.

"Uh!" he grunted, falling to his knees.

In desperation, I ran around him and flew up the stairs to the open door. I slammed it shut and locked it.

"Bitch!" he raged from down below.

Sobbing, I ran through the small house and out the door.

Chapter Twenty-four

Reed

"Where is Sinclair?" I asked Jesse, passing him outside of the library. I was exhausted and had just spent the last hour arguing with Sela until she'd finally called a cab and left. As far as I was concerned, it was over. Fortunately, she didn't have many things at my condo in New York, so I could ship them to her place instead of having to deal with any further tantrums.

Jesse ran a hand over his face and sighed. "I don't know. She doesn't have her cell phone, and the last time I saw her was with that Pastor Richie guy."

I frowned. "What was she doing with him?"

"The valet attendant said she followed him out to his car because he had an anniversary gift or something."

I raised my eyebrows. "And she hasn't been back yet?"

"I know," he said. "It doesn't make sense. The valet said he was talking to another guest and didn't realize they'd left until the Pastor's car was already gone."

"So both of them are missing?"

Jesse nodded. "Apparently."

"Why in the world would she leave with him? I just don't understand."

"I don't either. It's not like her, at all."

"Hmm... have you seen mother lately? Maybe she knows something about it."

"I'm here," she called from the top of the stairs. She was swaying slightly and looked slightly disheveled.

"Are you okay?" I asked, climbing the steps.

Mimi smiled weakly. "Oh, I've been better. I found out about Jack's little scene over by the pool tonight."

I sighed. "I'm sorry about that, mom."

She wiped a tear from her cheek. "You have *nothing* to apologize for," she sniffed. "He's gone too far this time."

I cocked an eyebrow. "This time?"

"Yes, I know... he's a *scoundrel*. You can't always choose who you love, and it certainly isn't easy to love a man like that."

"I know, mother," I said, hugging her. It was the same speech I'd heard growing up. She would complain but never leave. "Just remember, if you need us for anything – support, money, a place to stay, Jesse and I are always here for you."

She nodded. "Thank you, dear."

"Not to change the subject," I said as she dabbed at another tear. "But, would you happen to know where Pastor Richie has gone? Apparently, he and Sinclair left together quite a while ago, and neither has returned."

"What?" she asked. "Why in the world would she leave with *him*?"

I told her about the gift.

"Gift? I sent him home after I'd decided not to renew our vows. He never mentioned anything about giving us a gift," she said.

"Do you have his phone number?" I asked.

She frowned. "Well, he called me this morning around nine o'clock on the home phone. We can see if it's been saved."

"Okay," I said. "Jesse, go check the Caller ID and find that number."

He nodded and left.

"How do you know this pastor, anyway?" I said. "Do you go to his church?"

She shook her head. "No, actually I've never spoken to him before in my life. He told me that a friend of the family suggested he call us to see if we wanted to renew our vows, since we were having a big anniversary party. I thought it was a lovely idea and just agreed."

I frowned. "So, you don't know which church he's from or where he came from?"

"Well, he mentioned a church, but I forgot the name. He's a man of God; surely you don't suspect anything foul?"

"Fuck, I hope not."

She tilted her head. "Language."

"Sorry."

We went in search of Jesse and he was perplexed when we found him in the kitchen playing with the phone.

"It looks like someone erased the call logs," he said.

"You're kidding me," I said. "What in the hell is going on here?"

Jesse bit his lower lip. "I don't know but Sinclair would never have taken off like this. Not without letting me know about it. Something is very wrong here."

"And mother doesn't really know this Pastor Richie, either," I said. "For all we know, he could be some criminal off of the streets, who may have kidnapped her."

"Oh," cried Mimi, putting a hand to her lips. "Do you think so?"

"I don't know but I think we'd better search the property again, and if we can't find her, get the police involved," I said. "That's what I think."

Chapter Twenty-five

Sinclair

I stumbled through the dark woods, not sure of where exactly I was or which way I needed to go. My head was throbbing, and my bare feet were bleeding from the sticks and rocks I couldn't see in front of me, but felt every step of the way.

Where the hell am I?

From the shadows of mountains peeking over the trees, I knew one thing was certain; I was not *anywhere* near Huntington Beach anymore.

This realization was hard to swallow, but after escaping the clutches of the perverted pastor, I was happy to just be alive.

You can do this, I told myself as my side began to ache. *Just keep moving.*

I pushed on.

***

Reed

"You have his license plate number?" I asked the valet for the second time.

He handed me a clipboard. "Yeah, it's right here. We write down each one, in case there are problems. See, the signature? I parked his personally."

I scanned the information. "Great, thanks."

"Something wrong?" the kid asked.

"I hope not. Did the woman leaving with him seem nervous or frightened at all?"

He shook his head. "No, they were very friendly. In fact, she held on to his arm as they walked down the street."

"Did you see her get into his car?"

He shook his head. "No, I didn't. One of the other guests came out for a cigarette, a blond with long legs, and I stopped paying attention to the other two."

"Well, thanks for the help," I said. "Stick around here in case we need to get the police involved."

He nodded vehemently. "Yeah, no problem. I hope that lady is okay. She was something else, you know what I'm saying?"

"Oh, I know what you're saying," I answered, grabbing my cell phone. I dialed a number on my contact list – an ornery New York cop who was also one of my best friends.

"Benny, it's me," I said into the phone.

"What the hell? Do you know what time it is?" he grunted. "Jesus Christ."

"Yeah, I know. I'm sorry but it's an emergency."

He snorted. "It's always an emergency with you. Let's hear this particular one."

I chuckled. "What's wrong? Jenny cut you off again?"

"I got a piece yesterday, asshole. I'm just fucking tired. It's late."

"I can tell."

"Come on, I don't have all damn morning. What's the story?"

I gave him a rundown of what I knew and he sighed. "Okay, the car could be stolen but let me make some phone calls and see what I come up with."

"Thanks, Ben. I owe you."

"Damn right you do."

I hung up and went to go find Jesse to see if he'd heard anything yet.

***

Sinclair

When I finally cleared the woods and stumbled upon a dirt road, I was so relieved I almost started crying. I knew I wasn't out of the clear, but surely this road would lead to someone who could help me.

It had to.

I pushed on and on until the sun peeked over the horizon and the dirt road finally led to one with pavement. After another thirty minutes or so of walking, I saw a gas station in the distance and it gave me the adrenaline I needed to get me there.

"Holy shit," said the old woman behind the counter as I limped into the store. Both of my feet felt like they were on fire.

"Where am I?" I asked.

She looked at me like I was high. "What do you mean, where are you?"

"Please, what city is this?"

"You're in Big Bear Lake."

That was almost two hours away from Huntington Beach.

"Call the police," I said, knowing I probably looked like hell. My hair was now a tangled mess, my mascara was probably all over my cheeks, and my expensive designer dress – it was ruined.

"You hurt?" she asked, staring at me. "You want me to call an ambulance?"

I shook my head. "No, just call the police for now. Please," I said.

As she reached for the phone, I noticed a car pull up to the station. When I recognized the model and the driver, my heart stopped.

"Oh, my God," I choked. "That's the man who kidnapped me. Call the police, hurry!"

"Pastor Michael?" asked the woman, staring back at me in shock. "Why surely he would never..."

"He did this to me!" I hollered, spreading my arms out. "Please, call the police!"

"But..."

"Fuck," I said, annoyed that she didn't even believe me. "Just don't tell him about me when he gets inside. Please."

She frowned. "Well, all right."

I raced to the back of the store and locked myself into the bathroom, which smelled like sewage and stale cigarettes. I waited, wondering if he'd seen me walk into the station and if so, what he'd do. I closed my eyes and leaned against the door, praying that he'd just go away and I could get help.

A few minutes later, when the handle to the bathroom began to jiggle, I choked back a terrified scream and backed away from the door.

"Hello?" called the woman from the counter. "Miss?"

I sighed in relief. "Is he gone?"

"You can come out now. You're safe."

I unlocked the door and stepped warily out of the bathroom.

"Come on now," she smiled, beckoning me with her hand. "Let's get you something to drink."

"Thanks," I said, following her to the front of the store. When we reached the counter, I gasped in horror.

"Hello, Sinclair," smiled Pastor Richie, wearing his disguise once again.

"Oh, my God!" I cried, backing away. "You lied to me!"

"Calm down, miss," said the woman. "Pastor Michael explained everything. You're going to be fine."

I shook my head vehemently. "No, he's crazy. He tried raping me!"

Pastor Richie took a step towards me, his hands raised. "It's okay, honey. You're confused. You know that I would never hurt you. Now, come with me and we'll find your pills, then everything will be okay." He turned to the cashier. "She went out last night and didn't take her meds, now her parents are frantic with worry."

"No!" I hollered. "He's lying. Please, call the police!"

The woman frowned and reached for the phone. "Well, I think that maybe I should call the police, Pastor. They might have better luck calming her down."

He sighed and reached behind his back. "I'm truly sorry about this, Cindy," he said, pulling out a gun.

"Oh, my God!" gasped the cashier.

"No!" I cried, as he pointed the revolver at Cindy and shot her in the face without any hesitation.

"This was your fault," he said, now aiming the gun at me. "You've ruined everything, you know."

I raised my hands. "I'm... I'm sorry. Please don't shoot me," I sobbed.

His face softened and he opened his mouth to say something, but then a man stepped into the store, startling the both of us.

"What the hell?!" hollered the customer.

"Run!" I screamed.

As Pastor Richie aimed his gun at the shocked man, I turned and ran to the back of the store through a set of swinging doors.

"Oh, my God," I moaned as the Pastor's gun went off again. I couldn't believe how insane he was, killing those two without remorse.

"Come out, Sinclair!" hollered the Pastor. "We can work something out if you just quit resisting me."

Sobbing, I ran to the very back of the supply room and found an outside exit. I opened it and began limping away from the station, towards the forest. Just when I reached the cover of the trees, someone grabbed me around the waist and slammed me into the ground.

"Sinclair!" hollered the Pastor. "Stop!"

"No!" I cried, struggling to get away.

"Settle down," he said, turning me over. "We have to get out of here."

I hit him and raked my fingernails across his face as he tried grabbing my hands.

"Stop this, Sinclair!"

I grabbed his hair and pulled so hard, he gasped in pain. As he tried to remove my hand, I reached down with the other one, wrapped my fingers around his crotch and squeezed.

"Bitch!" he howled, punching me in the chin.

My face was on fire as he rolled away, but it didn't stop me from trying to escape. I crawled away from him, got up, and started running back towards the road. When I saw a squad car pull in to the parking lot, I cried out in relief.

Chapter Twenty-six

Reed

"The car was stolen?" repeated Jesse in horror. "Who in God's name *is* this freak?"

"I don't know," I said, sitting down next to him in the dining room. "The cops should be here shortly. Maybe they'll know something more."

"I'm so sorry," sobbed Mimi as she wiped her eyes with a tissue. "I had no idea he was lying to me. No idea."

"Mom, obviously we were all duped. It could have happened to anyone," I said, especially to someone as gullible as her.

Jesse ran a hand through his hair, making it stick up in disarray. "What in the hell did he want with Sinclair?"

"Oh, God," moaned Mimi. "I hope he doesn't rape her. The poor thing."

That had been my first thought, but hearing it spoken out loud was enough to make me want to kill the bastard who took her several times over. "Did she ever mention anyone stalking her or threatening her?" I asked Jesse.

Jesse shook his head. "No. Never. She doesn't go out much, she isn't dating anyone, and she pretty much keeps to herself."

Mimi's eyes narrowed. "I thought she was dating you?"

Jesse sighed. "We're just friends, mother."

Mimi leaned forward. "But I thought..."

"Jesus Christ," I said. "You already know the answer to that. Quit lying to yourself."

"I don't know what you mean," said Mimi.

"I'm gay, mom!" snapped Jesse. "Open your eyes."

She opened her mouth but no words came out.

"Congratulations," I said. "You should have announced it a lot sooner, though, don't you think?"

Jesse didn't say anything, he just stared at the fireplace in despair.

"It'll be okay," I told him. "We'll find her."

"I hope so," he mumbled. "Sinclair doesn't deserve this. She's my best friend and I don't know what I'd do without her."

***

The cops showed up sometime after three in the morning and questioned us along with the valet who'd watched her leave with the pastor. After filling out a report and making a final search of the premises, they prepared to leave.

"That's it?" I asked. "Isn't there more you can do?"

One of the men, a young officer named Drake, who looked to be around Jesse's age, shrugged. "There isn't more we really can do at this point. She hasn't even been missing for twenty-four hours."

"But there's foul play involved," I said. "She may be dead in twenty-four hours."

"Are you sure this friend of yours didn't know the perp?" asked Drake.

"No, absolutely not," said Jesse.

"Have you checked around to see if anything of value is missing?" asked the other officer. "The guy is obviously a thief."

"The only thing valuable missing is Sinclair," I snapped.

"Listen," said Drake. "We'll look into everything you've given us and get back to you. For now, I'd call her family and friends, to see if she's been in contact with them."

I nodded. "Okay, fine. But call us if you find out anything."

"Will do," said Drake. "We'll check the phone company's records, too. See if it brings us anything."

"Okay," I said, although the odds were that the cell phone he used was probably stolen, too.

***

Reed

I couldn't sleep. All I could do was pace around the house and stare outside, wondering where the hell Sinclair was. It wasn't until the sun finally rose and I had coffee in my system that I decided to try searching for her myself. I had no idea where to start, but I couldn't sit around the house and just do nothing. I grabbed the keys to my car and started towards the front door when Jesse stopped me.

"They found her!" he hollered. "She just called me. She's okay."

I sighed in relief. "Thank God. Where is she?" I asked.

"Midway Hospital," he said. "She has some minor bruises, but she's doing fine."

"Thank God," I said. "Let's go."

Chapter Twenty-seven

Sinclair

"You have visitors," said the nurse, an older woman with kind blue eyes and salt and pepper hair.

I cleared my throat. "My parents?" I knew they were supposed to arriving within the hour.

"No, your fiancé and his brother," she said.

I raised my eyebrows. My *fiancé?*

"Okay," I said, sitting up straighter in the bed, realizing who it had to be.

A few moments later, Jesse breezed through the door with Reed following close behind, each carrying a bouquet of flowers.

"Oh, my God, *Sin*," said Jesse. "Are you okay?" he asked, grabbing my hand. "I was so freakin' worried about you."

"I'm fine," I answered softly. "Now, that is."

Reed moved closer to my bed and his face darkened. "Did he do that to your face?" he asked with at tight jaw.

I touched my chin, which was still very sore. "Yes," I said. "But I'm sure that I hurt him much worse."

"Good," said Reed, relaxing slightly.

"So, what happened?" asked Jesse.

I told them everything, including the fact that I'd cut the psycho man's hair a few times and his obsession with me.

"Did they catch him?" asked Jesse, chewing on his lower lip.

I shook my head. "No, unfortunately he escaped and they're still looking for him."

"You're kidding," gasped Jesse. "He's still *at large*?"

I nodded. "Apparently. They traced him back to the cabin where he'd held me, but I guess it's not even his place. He must have broken in."

"What about fingerprints?" asked Reed.

"I'm sure they'll get some," I said. "So, at least there's that."

"We were so worried about you," said Jesse, touching my hair with tenderness. "Not knowing what had happened."

"It was pretty scary," I said.

"Jesse," said Reed. "Could I have a minute alone with Sinclair?"

Jesse stood up. "I don't know, can I trust you?" he joked.

"You can but she might not be able to," said Reed.

I had to refrain from rolling my eyes. The fact that I'd almost interrupted him and Sela having sex in the library still angered me. I didn't even want to hear his excuses.

"I don't know, seeing how Sin escaped one crazy bastard, I think you're the one who should be careful," smiled Jesse, as he stood up and walked towards the door.

"I hear you," said Reed, sitting down next to me.

The intensity of his gaze was disarming and I knew I had to get rid of him. I just didn't have the strength to deal with his lies at the moment.

"Reed," I said after Jesse had left. "Look, I'm really tired and would just like to rest if you don't mind."

He raised his eyebrows. "Are you kicking me out?"

I licked my lips. "Well, I'm grateful that you stopped by to check on me, but I'd just like to be alone for a while, until my parents show up. You know?"

He sighed and rubbed his hands over his face. "I understand. I'm sorry, I just wanted to –"

"Please," I interrupted. "We can talk later, okay?"

He nodded and stood up. "Okay. How long are you going to be in the hospital?" he asked.

"They're keeping me overnight and then my parents are going to take me home tomorrow morning."

"I could drive you."

I shook my head. "No, thanks."

He frowned. "Can I at least *call* you?"

"Um, sure. Jesse has my number."

His eyes narrowed. "Why do I have this feeling that you're brushing me off?"

Because I am?

"That's ridiculous," I lied. "I'm just exhausted and after everything that's happened..."

"Okay, sure, I understand. Well, I'll definitely be calling you, if that's okay?"

"Sure," I said, wondering how Sela would feel about that. Obviously he wouldn't tell her.

He bent down and brought his face next to mine. "I'm sorry that this happened to you," he said, his voice low. "If you need anything –"

"I'm fine," I answered.

"*Anything*," he continued with a stern voice. "You call me. You still have my card?"

I nodded. "I'm sure it's with my things back at your parents' home."

"Actually, Jesse brought your overnight bag, it's in the trunk."

"Okay."

His eyes softened and he leaned forward as if to kiss me, but I pulled away. "Please, my entire face aches."

Reed's eyes burned into mine before he raised his lips and kissed the top of my head. "Take care of yourself," he said. "I *will* call you."

Right. Only when his fiancée was out of town and he wanted a piece of ass.

"Okay," I said.

***

Reed

I wasn't sure what was going through Sinclair's mind after everything she'd been through, but I could definitely tell she was distancing herself from me. I wasn't going to press her about it, however.

Not yet.

I went back out into the parking lot, grabbed her overnight bag, and brought it back to the room as Jesse was saying his goodbyes.

"I'll call you," I said, trying to control the rage I felt inside from seeing her beautiful face so bruised and swollen. I wanted to find that bastard myself and fuck him up.

Bad.

Make him pay for what he'd done to Sinclair.

"Okay," replied Sinclair, not quite meeting my eyes.

Sighing, I took one final look at her before I left the room. She looked so small and vulnerable in the hospital bed and I wanted nothing more than to stay and protect her. The fact that she was pushing me away was aggravating. but I certainly couldn't be angry with her. She'd been through hell the last few hours.

"Keep your chin up," I said. "And call me if you need to talk."

She nodded, although it looked as if she'd already given up on having anything further to do with me. Little did she know that *I* didn't give up that easily.

Chapter Twenty-eight

Sinclair

When my parents arrived at the hospital, they were obviously upset and I had to keep reassuring them that I was fine.

"You're coming to stay with us until they catch this person," said my mother, her eyes brimming with tears. "Promise me, Sinclair."

"Mom," I said, squeezing her hand. "I'm not going to let this man scare me, okay? I have a job and a life. I can't let him take that from me."

"Then we'll hire a bodyguard for you," said my father, clasping his hands in front of his round belly.

I stared at him and smiled, so happy to see them, again, even under such crazy circumstances. My parents were in their sixties and remind me of what Santa and Mrs. Claus would look like if they'd retired in Stanton – both short, round and tan with laugh lines, pug noses, and puffy white hair. My dad even had a little white beard and smokes a pipe now and again.

"You don't have to do that," I said.

He frowned. "Well, the police should assign one for you. That's why we pay our taxes, isn't it?"

"The detective I spoke with earlier said they'd probably do that," I said. "Especially now that's he's killed two people. They're going to send someone to talk to me again, tomorrow before we leave the hospital."

My mother gasped. "Are they worried he'll come looking for you?"

I sighed. "Well, they *think* he's probably taken off, fled the city, but they don't know for certain."

My dad nodded. "They'd better get someone for you because I don't want you going *anywhere* unescorted."

"Dad..." I said.

"No, I'm serious. If I have to follow you around everywhere myself, I will," he said.

Just then, a nurse knocked on the door and stepped inside. "The detective from earlier is back to see you," she said.

"Good, send him in," said my dad. "I want to talk to him about security, find out what they plan to do."

I sighed. "Dad..."

"Dad nothing," he said, bending down to pat my hand. "You're my little jewel and I'm not going to let anyone threaten you again. Not if I can help it."

My awesome dad had called me that since I was a baby. *His little jewel.* I smiled up at him.

The bald detective from earlier stepped into the room, his face much less grim than earlier. He held out his hand to my parents and introduced himself.

"Have you heard anything about this monster?" asked my dad. "Have you people found him, yet?"

The officer smiled. "Actually, that's why I stopped back here myself, to tell you the good news."

"Good news?" I asked, sitting up straighter.

He nodded. "Well, it appears that your attacker was killed in an automobile fire a couple of hours ago."

"Are you serious?" I asked, shocked.

He pulled out a small pad of paper. "Yes, there was an accident involving a semi and a sedan that we believe the perp was driving at the time. The car flipped over the side of a ravine and then started on fire."

"And you think it's him?" asked my father.

"Well, the man was burned pretty badly but we found some forged IDs he'd hidden in a small safe in the trunk which, fortunately for us, survived the fire. One of the IDs was for a 'Michael Richie'."

"Oh, my God, it had to be him," I said.

"Well, we believe it is. We're still investigating the scene and do not really know his true identity yet, but I thought you should know," said the detective.

"Tell us, detective, do you think it was really him?" asked my dad.

He nodded. "Personally, yeah I do. There was also a shitload of money and a prescription for Clozapine in the safe."

"What's Clozapine?" I asked.

"It's used to treat Schizophrenia," he said.

Now *that* made sense.

"He's really dead..." I murmured, feeling as if a great weight had been lifted from my chest. I could suddenly breathe again.

"As far as I'm concerned," replied the detective. "Your nightmare is over."

Chapter Twenty-nine

One Month Later

Sinclair

"Well, what do you think?" I asked Jesse as he stared at his reflection in the mirror. We were at the salon and I'd darkened his hair, this time with chocolate and caramel lowlights that really flattered his new windswept style.

He smiled. "Have to hand it to you, Sin, you know how to bring perfection up another notch. It looks *magnifico*," he said, kissing the tips of his fingers.

I laughed and removed the plastic cape from his shoulders. "I'm sure Daniel is going to love it."

Daniel was his new Asian boyfriend. He was also gorgeous, young, and full of energy. They'd met three weeks ago at a club and were almost inseparable. Fortunately, we'd gotten to know each other a lot better the day before when I'd given him a trim. He was totally digging Jesse and the feeling seemed to be mutual.

"Oh, I know he will," he said, his eyes sparkling with excitement. "We're flying to Vegas tonight. I told you, right?"

"Only about ten times," I said. "You two have fun and make sure to behave yourselves."

He snorted. "Vegas is no place to behave, sweetheart. I plan on being as naughty and obnoxious as I can. Wanna join us?"

"Although I'd love to tag along and witness your mischief, I'm going to decline. Thanks, anyway."

He put a hand on my shoulder and shook it playfully. "You really need to get out more, you know that, don't you?"

"I'm fine," I said. "I like my solitude."

He sighed. "So, I wasn't going to bring this up, but Reed says you still haven't been returning his calls"

"I told you *why*," I said, bending over to clean up the hair on the ground.

"You know he isn't with Sela, anymore."

"Yeah, but he's still a player and I'm not interested in dating that kind of guy."

Jesse smiled, wickedly. "You could just use him for sex."

"No way," I said. Although I couldn't say the thought hadn't entered my mind. Not after the way he'd affected me. I wasn't interested in getting my heart broken, however. A man like that would be too easy to fall for.

Jesse followed me up to the register where Felicia was ringing her last customer of the day.

"Hey, girl," said Jesse. "You're looking fabulous. Hot date tonight?"

Felicia had recently cut and bleached her hair super short, which flattered her large brown eyes and high cheekbones. Today, she was also wearing a purple form-fitting dress that emphasized her voluptuous body in a most sinful way.

"Football player," she smiled, proudly. "Grayson Parker Fields."

"No way!" gasped Jesse. "That man is so fine, he even gets me interested in football."

She laughed boisterously. "I hear that."

"You'd better watch out in that dress," said Jesse. "That 'Tall Drink of Water' is going to be throwing some passes tonight."

She put a hand on her hip. "Tell you the truth, it's only our second date but I'm hopin' he goes for a touchdown. He's was in field goal range last week and I had to block his punt, but baby, tonight I'm leaving the defense on the sidelines."

Jesse and I both laughed, although I had to admit, all of this talk was beginning to make my end-zone a little tingly, which made my thoughts drift back to Reed. Although he was a scoundrel, he sure knew his way around a woman's field.

"Listen, I've got to go," said Jesse. "You two women have great weekends," he kissed me on the cheek. "And you, dear friend, try to get out and have some fun. Quit holing yourself up in that damn apartment. Especially with that grouchy old cat of yours."

"I'll *think* about it," I said.

"See you around, Jesse," said Felicia as the door opened and our new owner stepped inside of the salon.

"Hi, Thane," said Jesse, raking over him with his eyes. "Love your shirt."

It was just a simple black polo shirt with the salon logo on it, but even I had to admit, on

Thane's firm, muscular body, it looked anything but simple.

"Hey, guys," said Thane, flashing a rare smile. "Wow, who's the lucky man you're going to knock the sox off of tonight, Felicia?"

She smiled. "I told you about Grayson," she said. "We have *another* date."

"That's right," he said, walking past us. "Well, have fun, but remember we open early tomorrow. Don't be late."

"How can I forget?" she said dryly. "I have to cut 'Old Man Henry' again in the morning."

I snorted. "He's back?"

"Yeah, you want him?" she asked. "He asked for me but you can have the perv if you'd like. He leaves big tips."

"Yeah, and slobber marks. No way, sorry."

"So, are you sure Thane is into women?" asked Jesse, still admiring him from afar.

Even I had to admit he was pretty cute. With his shoulder-length blond hair, chiseled face, and golden eyes, he reminded me of a lion, although, I still preferred the dark panther look of Reed, with his darker hair and icy blue eyes. It was too bad his den wasn't exclusive to just one woman.

"Oh, Thane is definitely not gay," said Felicia. "He's temperamental, egotistical, and wears steel-toed mountain boots. Plus, have you seen the way he watches Sera?"

I raised my eyebrows. "Sera, really?"

Sera, was our new nail technician. She was soft-spoken, skittish, and reminded me of a librarian with her constant severely knotted bun and thick glasses. She definitely *had* the potential to be drop-dead gorgeous, though, if she cared enough to go that route.

"Oh, yeah," said Felicia. "He definitely has a thing for that girl. Problem is, I don't think she realizes it. Sera quivers in fear every time he approaches her."

Maybe it wasn't fear that made her quiver, I thought, appreciating his firm buns when he bent down to pick something up off the floor.

"Too bad," sighed Jesse. "He is freakin' hawt."

"Hey, you're taken now, anyway," I scolded.

Jesse held up his hand. "Girl, do you see a ring on this finger?"

I shook my head. "You're exasperating."

"But you still love me," he laughed, walking towards the door.

"You know it. Have a great weekend."

"You too," he hollered, walking out.

***

Reed

"Where to?" asked the driver, as I stepped away from the airport and into the dry cab.

I gave him the address and unbuttoned my tie. It was just after nine o'clock in the evening and it was raining cats and dogs. My suit was damp and my stomach growled, but it was nothing compared to the hunger I needed to sate this night.

"First time out here?" asked the cabbie.

I stared out the window. "No," I said, not wanting to make conversation. Fortunately he picked up on that, because he didn't say anything for the rest of the trip. When we finally reached our destination, I gave him a healthy tip and stepped out of the cab, staring up at the worn building. The lime stucco-finished apartment building was old and, had probably seen much better days. Fortunately, the neighborhood wasn't too bad and the entrance was secured.

At least I'd thought.

"Did you need to get in?" asked a young woman, holding the door open for me. She was on her way out but from the appraisal in her eyes, she was thinking about following me back inside.

"Thanks," I said, surprised that she'd let a total stranger into the building. "Appreciate it."

"Certainly," she answered, her eyes staring into mine with a definite invitation. "So, you new here?"

"No, I'm just visiting a friend."

"Ah... is *he* new here?"

I laughed. "No, I think *she's* been here for a while."

"Oh," she pouted. "Well, if she ever moves on, look me up. I'm in apartment twelve."

She was pretty but didn't hold a flame to the woman I'd been obsessing over the last month. "I'll keep that in mind," I said.

Her eyes brushed over me one more time and she shook her head. "Lucky."

"I hope so," I answered under my breath as I walked up the steps towards my destination. When I stood outside of her apartment, I raised my hand to knock when the door opened from inside.

"Reed," she gasped.

"Sinclair," I said, looking into the eyes that had been haunting my dreams.

Chapter Thirty

Sinclair

While part of me was furious that he'd just showed up at my doorstep without being invited, another part of me was so giddy that I could hardly stand it. Yes, he'd pissed me off and I'd been trying to avoid him, but it didn't mean that I hadn't been obsessing about him almost every single day and night this last month. He was handsome, sexy, and a scoundrel, but I couldn't help but crave his touch.

"What are you doing here?" I asked, unable to stop staring. I wanted to memorize every inch of his perfectly chiseled face and drink in those icy blue liquid eyes before I kicked him back out to the curb.

His eyes skimmed my short black dress and heels, then his lips lifted into a seductive grin. "To see you. And I have to say, I really like what I see."

I ignored the butterflies in my stomach and folded my arms under my chest. "To see me? Well, I'm just about to go out."

His smile fell. "You are?"

"Yes, so you should probably leave. My date will be arriving in a minute."

My date was actually a guy I'd dated a couple of times before my last boyfriend – Shawn, one of my mother's friend's sons. He was kind of boring and always smelled faintly of peanut butter and cigarettes, but my mom had called me earlier this evening, begging me to go out with him, one last time. He'd just gotten dumped by his girlfriend and was depressed. I'd called him right after and talked him into meeting some of the girls from *Tangled* at a nearby nightclub for a few drinks, but that was all. The thought of him touching me made my skin crawl.

"Well, I took a cab," he said. "Can I come in and make a phone call?"

Raised my eyebrows. "Don't you have a cell phone?"

"Yes, but the battery died."

"Oh," I sighed. "Yeah, sure... come on in."

I turned away and he followed me into my apartment.

"Nice place," he said. "Your apartment is quite a surprise compared to the outside of the building. I like it."

Most of the money I earned went towards my eclectically-furnished apartment, from my Italian leather furniture and large plasma television to the hand-carved dining set that I'd purchased from the Amish. Recently, I'd also acquired a couple of abstract paintings from a nearby gallery, which reminded me of my trip to Huntington Beach. I was rather proud of my diverse decor, so his complement put a smile on my face.

"Thanks," I said, pointing towards the phone. "I have to finish getting ready."

Just then my cat, Felix, strutted out of my bedroom to check out my guest.

"Here, kitty," said Reed, holding out his hand.

Felix stared at him but didn't move any closer.

"He's a little moody," I said. "I'd just leave him alone."

"Oh, usually cats love me," said Reed as he took a step closer to Felix.

The cat hissed at him.

"Sorry. He's old and doesn't like other men invading his space," I said.

"I see that. How long have you had him?"

"For almost fifteen years. My parents gave him to me when I turned nine."

Felix let out a low growl as Reed tried to pet him.

"I'd just let him go on his way," I said. "He's a grumpy old man."

"No kidding."

"Go back to bed if you're going to be crabby," I said to the cat.

Ignoring me, he walked into the kitchen to check on his food dish, which I'd filled before Reed had knocked.

"So, who is the lucky man?" he asked, sitting down on my sofa.

I grabbed a brush out of my purse and began running it through my hair. "This guy I dated before my ex."

"So, if he obviously wasn't the one then, why would you waste your time with him now?"

"It's just a date," I said. "I'm not looking for anything long-term."

He watched me brush my hair, his expression unreadable. "Sinclair, why wouldn't you return any of my calls?"

I stopped brushing. "I've been really busy."

He stood up and walked towards me. "Is that so?"

I took a step back. "Uh, yeah."

His lip twitched. "It's funny but I have this crazy notion that you've been avoiding me."

"Oh?"

"But that wouldn't make sense, would it?"

I opened my mouth to say something, but then recognized the look in his eyes.

Determination.

He licked his lips. "Because we never finished what we started and I'm pretty sure both of us wanted to."

I thought about the way his tongue had felt on my inner thighs and my pulse sped up. "Reed…"

He pulled me into his arms and crushed his lips to mine, invoking a small moan deep in my throat. Before I knew it, he was forcing his tongue inside, his strokes hot and demanding, creating a hot tingly sensation between my legs.

I moaned again and his lips moved to my earlobe. "Tell me to stop."

"Stop," I whispered.

Reed grabbed the back of my hair and wound it around his hand. He nipped the tender skin under my ear and then stroked it with his tongue. "You sure?" he asked, pulling me closer to his hips.

The only thing I was sure of was the power he had over my body. Every time he touched me, heat slid sinuously through my veins, there was an ache between my legs, and I couldn't breathe properly; the fact that I hadn't had sex in so long and my panties were drenched, didn't help matters.

"I can't stop thinking about you," he murmured, sliding his hands around the curve of my ass. "You haunt my dreams... your eyes, your mouth, your... smell. You smell unbelievable, did you know that?"

"No," I whispered.

"Well, you do. Like honey or vanilla, I don't know exactly what, but –"

I grabbed both sides of his head and brought his lips back to mine.

The man talked way too much.

From the way his tongue danced with mine, I knew he had much better things he could be doing with it. At the moment, talking definitely wasn't one of them.

"Um, wait," I murmured when his kisses stopped and he lifted me into his arms.

I started to panic.

Just like before, things were going a little too fast.

He looked around. "Where's your bedroom?"

"My date will be here any minute. We can't just disappear into my bedroom."

He found it and pushed the door open all the way with his foot. "Fuck your date."

"My friends are expecting me."

He set me down on the bed. "I'm sure your friends will get over it."

"But..." I said, backing away.

With a devilish smile, he removed his jacket and crawled towards me. "You're *mine,* tonight, Sinclair," he said. "Face it."

"I..."

He pushed me down on my back and his mouth devoured my protests until they were just meaningless whispers. I closed my eyes and decided it was going to be more rewarding to just give in.

Sensing my lack of resistance, he lifted the hem of my dress, pushing it up and over my hips.

"A thong," he groaned, into my mouth, sliding his fingers under the strap. His fingers followed the dark satin fabric over my hip to the front, lightly brushing the junction between my legs, making me tremble.

"Oh, wait," he murmured, stopping abruptly. He grinned smugly. "You told me to stop, didn't you?"

Quivering with need, I grabbed his hand and put it between my legs. "Don't."

"The lady has spoken," he whispered, as he slipped two fingers inside of my panties.

"Yes," I whimpered, as his thumb began stroking my swollen clit softly and then faster in a forceful rhythm. Then, when he dipped his other finger inside of me, I dug my nails into his shoulders.

"Oh, God," I moaned, as his fingers worked together, driving me crazy with desire. Just when it became too much and I was about to go over the edge, he stopped.

"That's cruel," I whispered.

"Patience," he chuckled, reaching around the back of my dress to unzip it. He pushed the spaghetti straps away from my shoulders exposing my black satin pushup bra. He cupped my breasts with his hands and lowered his mouth to my cleavage, running his tongue along the curves.

I slid my hands into his hair and closed my eyes as he unclasped my bra and tossed it away from the bed.

"You're so beautiful," he whispered, cupping them again. He squeezed and drew my right breast to his mouth, claiming the nipple between his teeth as his tongue rolled and teased it.

Crazy with need, I reached down to his trousers and clutched the outline of his hard cock, desperately wanting it out of his pants and inside of me.

He had other plans, however, because he grabbed both of my hands and placed them over my head. "Let me finish what I started," he whispered, staring at me with hooded eyes.

I nodded.

He released my hands and removed my dress, tossing it aside. Then his mouth returned to my nipples, nipping and sucking, causing hot currents all the way down to my clit.

"Perfect breasts," he murmured, giving them each one last kiss. Then his tongue began to move south, past my ribcage and bellybutton, until I could feel the heat of his breath on my thighs. When his tongue slid across my glistening lower lips, I gasped in pleasure.

Oh...

I reached up and grabbed the edge of my bed as his tongue began to lick, slowly and deliberately.

"Yes..." I moaned as his strokes became more urgent and one of his fingers slipped inside of me, followed by another. Soon he was sucking and licking with such intensity that it didn't take long before my body stiffened up and I screamed out his name, the force of my orgasm actually bringing tears.

"You okay?" he asked, noticing my glassy eyes.

I laughed. "Yeah, it's just been a while, I guess. I wasn't prepared for something that intense."

He got up and removed his shirt. "Well, we're not done yet."

I stared at his perfectly sculpted chest and narrow waist, waiting in anticipation for him to remove his pants. When he finally got down to his boxers, I couldn't take it anymore.

"Let me," I said, getting on my knees.

He smiled and moved until he was standing in front of me, his cock straining to get out of his shorts. I grabbed ahold of his boxers and pulled him closer until I was at eyelevel with his bellybutton. Licking my lips I moved closer and flicked my tongue just above the waistband of his shorts, teasing his lower stomach.

He sucked in his breath and grabbed the top of my head.

Smiling wickedly, I slipped my hand under the bottom of his boxers, lightly brushing his balls before I moved my hand up and took hold of his cock.

"Yes," he groaned as I began sliding my fingers up and down the shaft. The look on his face told me it wouldn't take long for him to come.

Wanting to get closer, I removed my hand and then pushed his boxers down his thighs, reveling at my first full glimpse of his beautifully sculpted cock. As I wrapped my hand around the middle and brought him to my lips, Reed groaned and put his hand on the top of my head.

"Sinclair," he whispered, his eyes glazed over with desire.

I stared up at him as I began circling the tip with my tongue, licking around the base. When I drew all of him inside of my mouth and began sucking greedily, he pushed me back against the bed.

"I have to get inside of you," he said, crawling between my legs.

Before I could respond, he had his cock pressed against my opening and was slowly pushing himself in.

"Sinclair," he whispered, pressing harder. "Relax."

"Well, it's been a while," I said.

He grabbed my hips more firmly and then with one big thrust, plunged inside of me.

"Yes," I moaned, enjoying the way he filled me up. It was a mixture of pain and pleasure as his hips began moving, his cock sliding in and out.

I stared up at him, marveling at how sexy he looked and how good he felt inside of me as he picked up his pace.

He lowered his mouth to mine and kissed my lips. "You feel so good," he whispered against my mouth. "I don't know how long I'm going to last."

"It's okay," I whispered, raking my nails across his back before I dug them into his ass, urging him on. "Just... don't... stop... now...."

He reached below and began rubbing my clit while he pumped in and out, making my toes curl back in ecstasy. Soon, my muscles clenched around his cock as another orgasm ripped through my body. Reed groaned and picked up his pace until his face twisted in pleasure and he pulled out of me.

"Sorry," he said, falling on top of me. "I should have worn something."

"Yes," I murmured. "If I get pregnant, I'm calling my lawyer."

He laughed. "Good."

Both of us lay there, still trying to catch our breath when the doorbell rang.

"I take it you didn't order a pizza and that's your date?" he said.

I groaned. "It's probably Larry. I'll tell him I'm sick or something."

He lay on his side. "Then get back here, because I'm not leaving this bed and I want you in it," he said, resting his head on his hand.

I stared at him as I put my robe on. I had to admit, he looked pretty good there. "Okay."

Fortunately, my date, Larry, was very understanding when I told him that I had a horrible case of diarrhea.

"Sorry, Larry. I'm sure it's something I ate but I wouldn't want to ruin your evening by being in the bathroom all night."

He looked slightly green. "No problem. Hope you feel better," he said, walking away, quickly.

Reed was sitting at the edge of my bed when I returned to my room.

"We need to talk," he said.

"Okay."

"Do you trust me?"

"I don't know," I said, being honest.

He grabbed my hand in both of his. "You can, Sinclair. I know we don't know each other very well, but I want you to know that *nobody* has affected me the way you have. Not Sela or any of the women I've dated in my life." He sighed. "I don't want to make you uncomfortable, but I think about you almost every minute of the day. When I'm in the courtroom, interviewing my clients, or even just trying to fall asleep at night. I'm officially obsessed with you, and that's a first for me; no joke. The only reason I waited to fly back out here was to give you some time."

"Oh." It was a lot to take in.

He raised my hand to his lips and kissed the side of it. "I was actually going to give you two months, but I got tired of waiting."

I smiled.

His eyes grew serious. "Jesse said that you were worried about me and thought I some kind of 'player'?"

I frowned. "He said you were definitely a 'ladies' man'."

He nodded slowly. "I'll be honest with you, I used to date, a lot, but that was long ago. I'm not that same person. I'm a one-woman man now. I just want you to know that."

I sighed. "Reed, what do you really want from me?"

He pulled me onto his lap. "I just want to be with you, get to know you, find out what makes you tick. Do you think you can let me do that? Maybe even return my calls from now on and let me see you?"

"You're saying all of these things but you live in New York and I live here. I don't know how that's going to work."

He smiled. "It just so happens that I'm moving back to Huntington Beach. Jack's been kicked out and I'm moving in with my mom temporarily, to help her figure things out. She needs the support."

"What about your career?"

"There are other law firms. I'm not worried about it."

I bit the side of my lips. "I guess we could see each other."

He began tickling my stomach. "You guess?!"

"Stop," I giggled as he got on top of me and held my arms over my head. "Yes, fine!"

Reed leaned down and kissed my lips. "I'd like to start right now," he said, pulling the belt away from my robe. "Seeing much more of you."

I bit his lower lip and then ran my tongue over it. "How about we see each other all night?"

He opened my robe. "How about all weekend? If you think you can handle it?"

"I'm willing to try," I said as his mouth found my right nipple.

"Tell you what – I'll lick your wounds, if it will help," he whispered, flicking and teasing it.

"My wounds?"

Leaving my breast, his mouth moved lower until his tongue reached a tender spot between my legs, where he spent the rest of the night kissing the soreness away.

Chapter Thirty-one

Michael

"Well, what do you think?" she asked, leaning down next to me as we both stared into the mirror.

"Magnificent," I murmured, drinking in her luxurious red hair and startling blue eyes. It was our first time together and I was giddy with joy.

Her pink bow-tie lips curled into a knowing smile that left me breathless. "I mean your new cut, Professor Jones. Do you like it?"

I chuckled. "Oh, of course. Yes, it's Jenna, isn't it?"

"It is," she answered, bending over to grab a small hand-broom.

I saw blue lace and a hint of cleavage peeking through her blouse as she swept up the leftover hair, and my cock twitched.

"Thanks for giving me a chance," she said, straightening up. "Being the new girl in the salon isn't always easy. I just moved here from Minnesota a couple of weeks ago and need to build up my clientele."

"Florida is a far cry from Minnesota. What brought you here?"

She looked away, but not before I noticed the pain in her face. She sighed. "I followed my fiancé out here."

"Oh, you don't sound very happy about that," I said.

Her smile was bitter. "Well, it didn't work out."

"I'm so sorry. I shouldn't have snooped."

"Don't be. Everything is fine. In fact, it all worked out for the best."

Yes, fate has brought you to me...

"Well, it was my pleasure and you did a fine job, young lady. In fact, I will definitely be back to see you again."

She smiled gratefully. "You will?"

"Oh, yes," I beamed. "There won't be anyone else for me, now that I've found you."

****

The End

www.ingramcontent.com/pod-product-compliance
Lightning Source LLC
Chambersburg PA
CBHW070020120726
47909CB00003B/1005